BREAK

"I think Barry has a special talent for tennis. All he needs is to be taught how to use it."

Tennis coach Frank Abbott may have faith in Barry Grieves' abilities as a tennis player, but few other people seem to agree. Games teacher "Muscles" Miller only encourages team games, pompous Major Houghton doesn't want "tearaways" at the tennis club, and Barry's father—who thinks that tennis is a snob's game—wants him to train for a steady job. There are problems all along the way—from lack of money to Barry's quick temper—but he's determined to become a tennis champion ...

BREAK POINT

Jeremy Burnham

BBC

BBC/KNIGHT BOOKS

To Paul Hutchins
National Team Manager of the Lawn Tennis Association
in the hope that fiction will become fact

First published by BBC/Knight Books 1982

British Library C.I.P.

Burnham, Jeremy
Break point.
I. Title
823'.914[J]   PZ7

ISBN 0-340-28084-0
(0-563-20046-4)

The characters and situations in this book are entirely imaginary and bear no relation to any real person or actual happening.

Printed and bound in Great Britain for the British Broadcasting Corporation, 35 Marylebone High Street, London W1M 4AA and Hodder and Stoughton Paperbacks, a division of Hodder and Stoughton Ltd., Mill Road, Dunton Green, Sevenoaks, Kent (Editorial Office: 47 Bedford Square, London, WC1 3DP) by Cox and Wyman Ltd., Reading

ONE

It was going to be a new record. He'd reached the top of Paignton Street—from where he could see the clock on St Mary's Church Tower—almost two minutes earlier than usual; and though he'd been delayed in Byfield Road, where Number Twenty-nine's flea-ridden mongrel had started snapping at his heels, he reckoned he was still over a minute ahead of his previous best time.

Barry knew these grey North London streets as a rabbit knows its multi-tunnelled warren. The area encompassed by his paper round was his "patch"—from the spacious, airy houses at the top of the hill to the squat back-to-backs at the bottom, in one of which, fourteen years ago, Barry himself had been born.

As a kid, this local knowledge had proved invaluable; when Mr Constantinou, the Cypriot baker, had caught him nicking the sausage rolls, when he'd been cornered by a group of drunken football hooligans, when the law had wanted to question him about the broken window at the Bank Street warehouse . . . On many occasions, the maze of side-streets and alleyways had been his sanctuary and his salvation.

Mr Ferris's newsagent's shop stood somewhere near the centre of Barry's "patch". So his paper round took him on a route shaped like a figure eight—looping down to the south, where they took the *Mirror*, the *Star* or the *Sun*, and up to the north, where they took *The Times*, the *Telegraph* or the *Guardian*.

Four years ago, when Barry had started his round, he'd varied his route to see if it made any difference to his time. Now he always did the northern section first: he'd learned from experience that it was better to tackle the uphill loop while he was fresh.

Gradually, over the years, he'd improved his time—until the most he could hope for was to shave it by a few seconds. But today, for some reason, he was way ahead of schedule, and the record looked like being shattered.

Perhaps it was this glorious early spring morning that made him feel so full of energy. Perhaps it was the thought of the whole summer spread out in front of him, the sight of St Paul's glinting in the sun, the prospect of his half-hour session in the park . . . Whatever it was, there was definitely something special about today; if he could run so much faster with no apparent effort, then anything was possible.

He dashed down Elm Street, hurdling the fences that divided each neat little garden from the next and turned into Ash Street. Only two to deliver here: the *Sun* to Number Eleven, and the *Mirror* to Number Thirty-five. Then just three more in Holmbrook Terrace, and he was finished.

Mr Ferris's bushy eyebrows arched up in surprise as Barry burst into the shop and leaned, panting heavily, on the counter. "Good grief!" he said, peering owlishly over his spectacles. "What are you trying to do? Kill yourself?"

"Whatsatime?" asked Barry, still gasping for breath.

Mr Ferris glanced at his watch. "Seven fifty-eight."

"I knew it." Barry grinned in triumph. "New record, that is. Sixty-five seconds inside the old one."

"Sure you did the full round?"

"Course. Record wouldn't be kosher if I'd skipped a couple of streets, would it?"

Mr Ferris frowned. "I'm not interested in records, Barry. All I'm interested in is my customers. How many of 'em got the wrong papers today, I wonder?"

"Leave it out, Mr Ferris." Barry looked hurt. "I may've made a few mistakes early on, but these days it's a doddle."

"Really? Forgotten about Colonel Hughes already, have you?"

"Eh?"

"Only three weeks ago, that little disaster. When you delivered the *Morning Star* to the Colonel, and the *Telegraph* to the squat in Dorset Gardens. They both nearly cancelled their orders."

Barry unhooked the green canvas bag from his shoulder and laid it on the counter. "They didn't, though, did they? 'Cos they get their papers quicker than anyone else in the manor. On account of I'm the fastest kid around."

Mr Ferris sighed heavily. "Yes, so you keep telling me. And the toughest. And the prettiest. And the greatest."

"Mohammed Ali never stopped telling people," said Barry, picking up a packet of chocolate raisins, "and look where it got him."

"Going to be World Champ, are you?"

"Yeh. But not at boxing."

Barry headed for the door, but Mr Ferris called after him: "Them chocolate raisins. I'll deduct 'em from your wages, right?"

"Right."

But Barry knew he wouldn't. Inside that dry old owl lay a soft heart, and both Barry and his father had cause to be grateful to him; the odd packet of chocolate raisins was a "perk" of the job, and since Barry's father had been made redundant three months ago, Mr Ferris had made sure he received his copy of the *Sun* as usual—without charge.

Back on the street again, Barry broke into a gentle jog, pausing every now and then to stuff another handful of chocolate raisins into his mouth. He was looking forward to this morning's session; he reckoned he could get in a good thirty-five minutes before school.

He'd told no one where he went after finishing his paper round. It was his secret, shared only with Old Sam, the park attendant. His school-mates would be sure to take the mickey if they found out, and his father would probably blow his top. "Waste of bleeding time," Barry could hear him saying, "no wonder your reports are so bad. Ought to be concentrating on your work, not messing about in the park."

But these early-morning sessions were the most precious part of his day—something to get up for, to look forward to. When things got too heavy at home—as they often did these days, with his father around all the time—he always knew he had an escape-hatch. There was always his own private corner of the world where he could be alone and at peace.

It had all started two winters ago, when he was wandering through the park after his paper round killing time till school. There had been a heavy frost, and Old Sam stood just inside the door of his hut, flapping his arms to try and keep warm. Barry knew him by sight—all the kids in the manor knew Old Sam—and waved to him. It was too cold to stop, so he hurried on, burying his hands deep in the pockets of his tartan lumber-jacket.

To his surprise, Old Sam called him back. "Hey—son . . ."

Barry turned, to see that the park attendant was beckoning to him. Reluctantly, he ran back to the hut.

"Fancy a cup of tea?" The old man's eyes were streaming with the cold. "I'm just brewing up."

Barry accepted the offer gratefully. He was frozen to the

marrow, and the prospect of having to face Mr Miller, his form master, while feeling like an icicle had filled him with foreboding. He still hadn't come up with an excuse for not doing his homework, and his brain wouldn't function till it had completely thawed out.

It was while he was sipping tea from a chipped china mug with a broken handle that he made a casual remark which was to change his life. Old Sam's hut stood next to the tennis courts, and Barry stared out at the six drooping nets, hanging like forlorn-looking flags at half-mast. "Don't look like you're going to get many customers today."

Old Sam took out a dirty handkerchief and blew his nose. "You never know. There's some idiots who'll turn up in any kind of weather."

"Just to hit a ball across a net? Must be off their nuts."

"You don't fancy it, then?"

"What—tennis? Do me a favour."

Old Sam shuffled to the back of the hut, and picked up an old racquet lying in a corner. "Ever tried it?"

"No. We don't have no courts at our school." Barry took the racquet and pinged the strings against his hand. Surprisingly, they felt quite taut. "And I can't afford to play nothing that costs money."

"You want to have a go?"

Barry frowned. "You mean—gratis?"

"Yeh." Old Sam reached up and took down a box from a shelf. "There's some old balls here you can use."

"Don't be funny. I can't play by meself."

"There's a practice wall at the back of the courts. Go and see if you can beat yourself."

So Barry started knocking up against the wall, and found to his surprise that he enjoyed it. He had always been good at games—though small for his age, he was tough and wiry —and played for the school Under-sixteen teams at both cricket and football. So, although it took him some time to get used to the bounce, his natural ball-sense soon taught him the rhythm of the game.

And there was something else he liked about it. On the cricket or football fields, he usually had to depend on someone else for his success—to catch the ball off his bowling, or to make the crucial pass when he was unmarked in front of goal. But here was a game in which he had only himself to blame if the ball didn't come back exactly as he wanted it.

Every weekday morning after that—winter and summer—Barry went down to the park as soon as he'd finished his paper round. Sometimes—if the papers were late—he would have only ten minutes to spare, but however short it was he never missed a session. He had no idea why, but it became a matter of honour with him.

After a few weeks of belting the ball harder and harder against the wall, Old Sam suggested he use one of the empty courts to practise serving. Barry had studied the other players, and learned that if you served from the right-hand side of the court, you had to get the ball into the little box just over the net on the *left*-hand side, and vice versa. That wasn't as easy as it looked, but he found that if you threw the ball up straight, you had greater control over it—and his speed and accuracy gradually improved.

And now, nearly two years later, he was in the curious position of having reached a high level of proficiency without having faced a single opponent across the net. But that, he told himself as he jogged down the path towards the courts, wasn't the point. One of these days, he might ask someone for a game, but not yet—not till he'd gone as far as he could on his own.

Old Sam was waiting for him at the entrance to his hut. "Court or wall?" he asked, handing Barry the same old racquet and balls.

"Court," said Barry, "I want to practise me high-kicker."

"OK—you can use Number Three. Only I'm expecting the guv'nor today. Could show up at any time. If he does, I'll have to charge you."

"Charge me? You can't do that, Sam—I'm skint."

Old Sam's leathery face creased into a smile. "Have to sub you, then won't I? Till Friday."

"Ta."

Barry ran on to the court and raised the net, checking the height against the measuring-stick. Then he walked back to the baseline and served six balls hard and fast into the right-hand service court, just inside the centre line.

He jumped the net, collected them from the stop-netting and prepared to serve again. This time, he threw the balls back over his head, and brought the racquet-head slicing across them. He had found that this method not only gave him greater control, but also imparted a vicious spin, causing the ball to kick sideways on landing.

He continued to serve from alternate ends, varying his deliveries to confuse his imaginary opponent. He reckoned that the receiver would be able to return only about one in three. He was so absorbed in his practice session that he didn't notice the two men who entered the adjoining court and stood watching him. One was tall, bearded, athletic; the other grey-haired, bespectacled and overweight.

They watched in silence as Barry served six balls into the left-hand service court with deadly accuracy. Then the bearded man turned to his companion. "You in a hurry, Mr Bousfield?"

Bousfield smiled. "No, Frank—I'm curious too. Go and do your thing."

The bearded man moved up to the stop-netting and called. "What's your name, son?"

Barry, in the act of picking up the balls, swung round,

startled. "I've paid, Mister," he said guiltily, "honest. Ask Sam."

"That's nothing to do with me. What's your name?"

"Barry."

"Like a knock?"

Barry stared at him suspiciously. "Why?"

"Thought you might like to practise some ground strokes. There's more to tennis than serving, you know."

Barry hesitated. Both the bearded man and his companion wore smart, expensive-looking track suits, but that didn't mean anything; there were plenty of players on the public courts who had all the fancy gear, but could hardly get the ball over the net.

"I'm pretty good, you know," he said cautiously. "No offence, Mister, but if you're a patball merchant, I'd sooner go on practising on me tod."

The bearded man shrugged. "Why don't we give it a try? If you reckon I'm not up to your standard, just say so."

"OK."

The bearded man opened the gate and held out his hand. "The name's Frank."

Barry took the hand awkwardly. "Hi," he said gruffly, to cover his embarrassment. He wasn't used to shaking hands.

Frank set his huge tennis-bag down on the bench and opened it. Barry stared in amazement. Inside were half a dozen racquets, which looked as if they'd hardly been used. There were four or five tins of tennis balls and several brand-new white shirts, still in their cellophane wrappers.

Frank selected a racquet, opened a tin of balls and tossed a couple to Barry. "Reckon you're pretty good, eh? Let's see if you're as good as you think you are."

They moved to opposite ends of the court, and began to rally. Barry felt exhilarated; his two years' regular practice against the wall had made him confident that he could cope with anything an average opponent could throw at him. After all, there weren't many blokes who could match a wall for steadiness and reliability.

He sent a few looping forehands across the net; easy stuff at first, to test the water. The returns looped back, at exactly the same pace and height. All right, thought Barry, he can cope with the slow balls: how about the fast ones?

He gradually reduced the trajectory, sending the ball lower and lower over the net and increasing his weight of shot. This didn't seem to worry Frank, who gradually increased the speed of his returns. Soon the ball was whizzing backwards and forwards across the net, and Barry was belting it as hard as he could.

Frank continued to play without apparent effort, returning Barry's best shots with almost contemptuous ease. The faster the ball came at him, the faster he sent it back.

Barry noticed that he hardly moved his feet, and that there seemed to be plenty of room to pass him on either flank. Probably too old to run about, he thought grimly; if I swing him from side to side, I'll soon wear him down.

So he started to drive for the corners—first the backhand, then the forehand. But he found to his dismay that as he increased the angle of his shots, the angle of the returns also increased, making them more and more difficult to reach. The irritating thing was that Frank seemed to anticipate exactly where each ball was going to land, so that he was always perfectly positioned long before it arrived. Without appearing to move, he covered the whole court, turning good length balls into volleys and half-volleys and putting Barry under more and more pressure.

Barry suddenly realised that *he* was the one being swung from side to side, that he was having to run faster and faster from corner to corner, and that consequently he could no longer put any weight into his shots; they became desperate, scrambled efforts that barely cleared the net.

He became more and more irritated. Frank looked old enough to be his grandfather, yet he was making him look a right berk. He gritted his teeth as he lunged for yet another sharp, angled backhand—no bearded wonder in a fancy track-suit was going to make a monkey out of *him*!

But just as he reached the ball, his right foot slipped on a loose stone and he lost his balance, crashing down heavily on the concrete and grazing his elbow.

He lay still for a moment, not badly hurt, but aware of the indignity of his position. Frank hurried up and crouched down beside him. "You OK?"

Barry sat up, gingerly feeling his elbow. "Yeh. Trod on a bleeding stone—otherwise I'd 've got it back."

"I'm sure you would." Frank picked up his racquet and handed it to him. "Probably turned it into a winner."

Barry glowered at him. "You taking the mickey?"

"No. You were right—you *are* pretty good."

"So are you," said Barry grudgingly.

"I should be. I make my living at it."

"A Pro? I should've known from the gear."

Barry stood up and started brushing the dust from his trousers. "Not torn, are they—at the back?"

Frank inspected the trousers closely. "No. Just a bit of dirt, that's all."

"Thank God for that. Me best pair, these are. Me Mum would've killed me."

They collected the balls, and Frank put them back in the tin. He clicked the lid in place, threw the tin in his bag—then turned to Barry. "Ever had any lessons?"

Barry shook his head. "Can't afford it."

Frank stared at him thoughtfully. "What time d'you finish school?"

"Half-three."

"You know the East Middlesex Club? In Lime Park Road?"

"Yeh."

"Meet me there at four. I'll give you a lesson—free of charge."

Barry frowned. "What's the catch?"

"Does there have to be one?"

"Yeh. Nobody ever gives something for nothing."

Frank bent down to zip up his tennis bag. "I just want to stretch you a little. Find out how much you know."

"Like an exam?"

"Sort of."

Barry didn't like the sound of this. "I don't usually fancy exams." Then, in sudden alarm as exams reminded him of school: "What's the time?"

Frank glanced at his watch. "Ten to nine."

"Got to go."

"See you at four, then?"

"OK."

Barry ran back to the hut, and handed the racquet back to Old Sam. He stood by the entrance for a moment, watching Frank and his partner begin knocking up. They looked fantastic in their immaculate track-suits, their brand-new steel racquets flashing in the sun. One day I'm going to look like that, he thought. Only I'm not going to waste it on public courts.

He turned to Old Sam. "That feller—the Pro. What's his surname?"

"Abbott. Frank Abbott."

"On the level, is he, Sam?"

The old man's eyes twinkled with amusement. "You mean is that his real name, or is he really a Pro?"

"I mean he's not like them salesmen? You know—the ones

that start off by handing you a free sample, and end up by flogging you Tower Bridge on the never-never?"

"Frank? No, he's not selling nothing. Why?"

"Just wondered if he was kosher."

"He's kosher all right. One of the best coaches in the country, they tell me."

"Who tells you?"

"People."

Barry was puzzled. "What's he doing here, then?"

Old Sam looked hurt. "You implying these courts is no good?"

"Course not. But if he's one of the best coaches in the country, why isn't he teaching at Wimbledon or something?"

"Search me." Old Sam took out some paper and tobacco and started to roll a cigarette. "Comes here quite a bit, though—usually later in the day. That's why you've never run into him before."

Barry stared across at the bearded man moving easily and gracefully round the court. "Frank Abbott, eh? Never heard of him."

"That makes you even. 'Cos I don't reckon he's heard of you neither."

Barry looked thoughtful. "He has now," he said, with quiet satisfaction. Then he turned and raced off down the path.

TWO

There was trouble brewing, he could sense it. All through the English lesson, Mr Miller had studiously ignored him—and that was a bad sign. He only did that when Barry had missed an open goal, or when he'd been out for a duck playing across the line.

For Mr Miller was also in charge of the Under-sixteen Football and Cricket teams. Barry had never liked him; he fancied himself too much, both as a muscle man and a games master. He seemed to spend all his spare time in the gym building up his physique, and he thought he knew all there was to know about tactics. They had lost several matches because he had given the team the wrong instructions.

And Barry was sure the dislike was mutual, that Mr Miller was only polite to him because he was one of the best players in both teams. For "Muscles"—as Mr Miller was known throughout the school—was only concerned with success, with the reflected glory that winning matches brought him. He wasn't interested in the boys who had no athletic ability, and he made his lack of interest only too obvious.

Barry despised him for that. To be good at games was just a matter of luck, and he didn't see why a boy's lack of ability should be held against him in the classroom. Yet there was no doubt that he and his team-mates received far more help and attention from Mr Miller than the others.

Today, however, was different—and he knew why. When he arrived at the school, he had found "Muscles" waiting for him in the playground. "Oh, Barry," he'd said, walking with him towards the classroom, "this match this afternoon. It's important we get off to a good start, so I want you to open the innings with Greg."

Barry stopped, turned to face him. "Sorry, Mr Miller. I can't make it."

Mr Miller frowned in disbelief. "Can't make it? But it's against Inglewood! We have to avenge last year's defeat."

"I got to meet someone at four. And Inglewood's halfway across London."

"Meet someone? Who?"

"A tennis Pro. He's giving me a lesson."

Mr Miller looked incredulous. "You arranged to play tennis? On a match day?"

"I didn't arrange it. He offered."

"Well, you'll just have to turn him down."

Barry looked down at his feet. "I can't—not now. I told him I'd be there."

"You had no right to tell him that!" Mr Miller's tone had become icy. "I'm sure I don't have to remind you that cricket is compulsory at this school . . ."

"School's supposed to finish at half-three," said Barry sullenly, "that's why I fixed it for four."

"You know perfectly well the match won't be finished by then. We'll be lucky to be back here by seven."

"I told you—I'm not playing. You can't force me to play."

Mr Miller contemplated him in silence for a moment. "That's true," he said quietly, "but if you refuse to turn out for the Under-sixteens, you'll have to take part in an ordinary pick-up game."

Barry shrugged. "That's OK. If it's here at the school, I can get away in time."

"Not if the game isn't finished, you won't. And certainly not if you're still batting."

"Have to make sure I'm out then, won't I?"

And that was how they'd left it. But Barry was sure it was only a temporary victory, that Mr Miller wouldn't let him get away with it as easily as that. "Muscles" wasn't the sort of man who accepted defeat: if he couldn't win by fair means, he wouldn't hesitate to try a foul.

"Wordsworth's poetry," he was saying, wandering down the line of desks, "can be summed up in one particular phrase, which we discussed last week. Anyone remember?"

Jason, a thin, freckled boy who was hopeless at games, put up his hand. Mr Miller gave him a light cuff on the back of his head. "Yes, I'm sure *you* know, Jason," he said dryly, "but I'm not asking our walking encyclopaedia. I'm asking the lesser mortals. What about you, Greg?"

Greg, a dark-haired giant who played centre back for the football team, shook his head. Mr Miller looked round the rest of the class. "Anyone else?"

No one volunteered. Mr Miller sighed, turned reluctantly back to Jason. "All right, Mastermind—tell 'em."

"'Emotion recollected in tranquillity,' sir," said Jason in his high, squeaky voice.

"Thank you."

The bell rang. There was instant pandemonium as the boys leaped up from their desks and raced for the door. But Mr Miller barred their way. "Sit down!" he roared. "Before you go, I have an announcement to make."

Here it comes, thought Barry. Whatever card "Muscles" had been keeping up his sleeve, he was about to play it. The boys moved back to their desks, and an expectant hush fell over the classroom.

Mr Miller mounted the dais and stared across the room at Barry, hands clasped behind his back. "I'm sure you'll all be disappointed to know," he boomed, "that Barry Grieves has decided not to play for the Under-sixteen Cricket team this afternoon. He tells me he has arranged a tennis lesson, which he apparently considers more important than helping the school defeat Inglewood ..."

He paused to let his words sink in, and several boys turned to regard Barry with puzzled hostility. Greg's expression was particularly malevolent, and Barry knew he could expect bother from that direction. Unable to shine in the classroom, Greg was a younger version of Mr Miller—an athlete who only came to life on the playing fields, where his size made him a formidable defender and fast bowler.

"I tried to persuade him to postpone his lesson," Mr Miller continued, "pointing out that he was deserting his team-mates in their hour of need ... but he refused. Though he couldn't explain why he wasn't prepared to rearrange it for another day ..."

Without turning his head, Barry was uneasily aware that Greg was whispering to Dennis, the team's wicket-keeper.

Mr Miller stepped down from the dais and walked slowly towards Barry, taking up a position just behind him. "Now those of you who played against Inglewood last year—our only defeat of the season, incidentally—will naturally have been thirsting for revenge. So you may feel like making one last effort to persuade Barry to change his mind. I hope you have more success than I did. Now you may go."

He strode quickly towards the door and went out. One by one the boys followed, glancing curiously at Barry as they left the room. Greg and Dennis brought up the rear, whispering conspiratorially to each other.

Barry remained at his desk, full of foreboding. That bleeder "Muscles"—he'd dropped him right in it! Now his team-mates would really put the pressure on—pressure which might well be physical. If he stuck to his guns, there was no way he could avoid a punch-up.

Well, if they were going to dish it out, he'd just have to take it. He wasn't going to back off now, wasn't going to lose his bottle in the face of this blackmail. They could do what they liked— but they'd never get him to change his mind. He stuffed his books into his bag, and walked slowly out into the playground.

As he feared, Greg and Dennis were waiting for him. "That true, Barry?" asked Dennis softly. "You're not going to play?"

Barry stared at him defiantly. Dennis was a pain—a stocky, chunky boy who fancied himself behind the stumps, but who had dropped three catches in the previous match. "Yeh," he said, trying to sound as if he couldn't care less what they thought of him, "it's true. So what?"

Greg started to wander round behind him. "Tennis lesson, eh? What's so important about a tennis lesson?"

Barry turned with him. Better to have Dennis at his back than this dangerous hunk. "Well for a start," he said warily, "it's free . . ."

Greg snorted contemptuously. "So if someone offered you a free dancing lesson, you wouldn't turn out for the team, right?"

"Tennis is different."

"Why?"

"'Cos it is—that's why."

Dennis's voice came from behind him. "If we lose, it'll be down to you."

"So?" Barry was still keeping Greg in his sights. "What's it matter?"

"It mattered when I dropped them catches last week," said Dennis menacingly, "and you gave me all them verbals."

Barry, forgetting about Greg for a moment, swung round to face him. "Yeh, well—I was playing then, wasn't I? Today I'm not—so you can drop as many catches as you like."

"You creep!" growled Greg in his ear. Barry felt a muscular arm tighten round his neck, slowly throttling him. "I'm going to keep squeezing till you promise to come to Inglewood."

Barry, unable to breathe, watched Dennis's grinning face swim out of focus. If he didn't do something quickly, he'd lose consciousness. Summoning up all his strength, he wrenched his head sideways and bit deep into Greg's forearm. Greg uttered a cry of pain, and his grip momentarily slackened. Barry ducked under his arm, and raced out of the playground. Once free, he knew he was safe—neither Greg nor Dennis were fast enough to catch him.

He didn't go into lunch, but hung around the school grounds till the bus had left for the match. Then he went down to the playing fields to report to Mr Frobisher, the elderly assistant games master, who ran the cricket matches for those not playing for the school.

"Ah—there you are," said Mr Frobisher as he saw Barry, "Mr Miller's had a word with me about you, Grieves. He says you're to go in Number eleven for the team batting last."

Barry was aghast. "But I told him—I gotta get away . . ."

"Sorry," said Mr Frobisher firmly, "Mr Miller gave me explicit instructions. Said you had to stay till the end of the match. So next time, maybe you'll think twice before letting the team down."

Barry felt himself flush with anger. If that was the way "Muscles" wanted to play it, he'd never turn out for the school again. He had no intention of missing his tennis lesson; it was the chance he'd been waiting for—and if they didn't like it, they could go and take a running jump. Tennis was much more satisfying than team games where they never gave you credit if your side won, and you always got the blame if it lost.

For an hour and a half he fielded on the boundary, where he had little to do. The ball seldom came near him, which gave him a chance to brood; Mr Miller was definitely out of order to cause him all this bother. He should be allowed to do what he like with his free time.

At the end of the opposing team's innings, he asked Jason the time.

Jason clicked on the dial of his new digital watch and studied it short-sightedly. "Three thirty-four and ten seconds."

Barry frowned; he was late! He looked round, saw that Mr Frobisher was busy writing down names in the score-book—dashed for the nearby bushes and disappeared into the undergrowth. If they were counting on him for a last-wicket stand, they were going to be disappointed; he had more important things to do!

*

He had passed the East Middlesex Club many times on his paper round. He had never been inside, considering it to be out of bounds to the likes of him. He had caught a glimpse of one or two expensive-looking cars in the car park, and several tennis-players dressed in immaculate whites; it was not his world, and if someone had told him that one day he would be invited to play there he would have thought they were out of their minds.

So he felt a little nervous as he stood in the gateway, surveying the eight, newly-raked hard courts basking invitingly in the afternoon sunshine. They looked so different from the park courts, where the nets were full of holes and the surfaces cracked and uneven.

There was no sign of Frank, so he made his way along the

path to the wooden building at the end which he assumed was the pavilion. He opened the door, poked his head inside; the place seemed deserted.

He went in and stood by the door, looking round. He found himself in a large recreation room, with a bar at one end—protected by a wire screen—and doors to the men's and women's changing rooms at the other. The centre of the area was occupied by a large ping-pong table, surrounded by comfortable-looking easy chairs. A fruit-machine stood by the far wall, next to a vast notice-board.

He wandered across and studied the notices. The Men's Team were apparently doing badly in their League, having lost the first three matches of the season. The Women, however, had fared better, with two wins and one loss.

According to the tournament-sheets, Mrs Potter, the top seed in the Ladies Singles, had reached the third round without losing a game; while A. Barnes, the top-seeded man, had obviously had quite a struggle in the second round, winning 7–5, 6–4.

There were notices advertising flats for rent, motor-bikes, record-players and second-hand racquets for sale. Members who wanted to be included in the draw for Wimbledon tickets were asked to put their names on a list. And several official reminders and warnings, typed on Club notepaper, were signed by "G. Houghton—Secretary".

Barry turned, walked round the ping-pong table and opened the door to the men's changing room. Rows of empty pegs, a smell of soap, and various articles scattered over the floor and benches—an odd shoe, two towels, a dirty tennis shirt, a soap dish . . .

Hanging on one of the pegs was a smart blue track-suit top, with white stripes down the sleeves. He took it down, carried it to a mirror and held it up in front of him. It was several sizes too large, but it suited him a treat. One of these days, he thought, when the prize money starts rolling in . . .

"What do you think you're doing?"

Barry turned, startled, to see a small brown man in a green blazer standing by the door. "Looking for Mr Abbott," he said, conscious that it didn't sound very convincing.

The brown man stared at him suspiciously. "You won't find him in here."

"Well I didn't know that, did I? I never been here before."

He hung the track-suit top back on the peg and headed for the door. But the brown man grabbed his arm and held it with fingers of steel. "Just a moment. You're one of Mr Abbott's pupils?"

"Yeh."

"Well let's make sure, shall we?" He started to propel Barry out of the room.

"Here—watch it. Who are you?"

"Major Houghton, the Club Secretary. And it's you I'm watching, young man. Because if you're not telling the truth—and I suspect you aren't—you and I are going to pay a little visit to the police station."

Barry tried to pull his arm away, but Houghton's grip was too strong. Giving up the struggle, he allowed himself to be hustled out of the pavilion, and along the path to the car park.

Frank was just climbing out of a battered Mini, accompanied by a small, dark-haired girl in tennis gear. Houghton called to him: "This one of yours, Frank?"

Frank frowned, obviously puzzled to see Barry being treated like a prisoner. "That's right, Major. I asked him to meet me here."

Houghton reluctantly released his grip. "Well I wish you wouldn't let him wander round the dressing rooms on his own," he said crossly. "Specially after the trouble we had with that Poskett boy . . ."

"Sorry." Frank moved up to them. "I intended to be here first—but I got held up."

"You're giving him a lesson?"

"Yes."

"But he's not a member."

Frank turned to the girl. "Lucy's agreed to sign him in as her guest."

Houghton stared at Barry with distaste. "And he's not wearing whites."

"Couldn't you stretch a point, Major? Just this once?"

Houghton chewed his lip thoughtfully. "All right—but if there are any complaints, I know nothing about it." He walked away, calling over his shoulder to the girl. "Don't forget the guest fee, Lucy. Leave it in my pigeon-hole before you go . . ."

Barry watched his receding figure with contempt. "Bleeding fascist! Should've stayed in the army."

"He could be useful, Barry—so be polite to him." Frank put his arm round the girl's shoulders and pushed her forwards. "This is Lucy Roberts—Britain's answer to Tracy Austin—Barry Grieves."

Barry eyed her warily. He didn't like what he saw; judging by her gear, she was one of the posh crowd—like the players he'd glimpsed through the trees on his paper round.

But she smiled pleasantly. "Who are *you* Britain's answer to?"

"John Travolta," he said sourly.

The smile faded. "Very funny."

They started to walk towards the courts. "I persuaded Lucy to share her lesson with you, Barry," said Frank. "She's agreed to let you have the first half-hour."

Barry didn't fancy having to owe the girl anything, but he realised it would be ungracious not to make some form of acknowledgement. "Ta," he said gruffly.

"Don't thank me. Frank twisted my arm."

"Ta all the same."

Lucy stopped and held out her hand. "Let's have the money, then. I'm not going to pay for you."

Barry glanced at Frank in alarm. If this was going to cost him, he'd have to scrub it. But Frank dug his hand in his pocket and produced two pound notes. He handed them to Lucy—who sniffed, then marched off towards the pavilion.

"I didn't know I'd have to pay," said Barry, wondering what he was getting himself into.

Frank smiled. "You don't."

"I mean—I didn't know *anyone*'d have to pay."

"Would it have made any difference?"

Barry shrugged. "Maybe not."

"Come on—let's try some volleys." Frank opened the gate to the courts, and Barry followed him through. The red shale crunched pleasingly under his sneakers, but he felt out of place. His school gear was good enough for the public courts, but not for a club like this. He hoped none of the members would turn up and complain.

Frank set his bag down by the net, opened it and handed Barry a steel racquet. "You can use this. Should be about your weight."

Barry banged the strings against his palm. They made a high-pitched pinging sound, very different from the old racquet he'd been using in the park. This time, he thought grimly, they'd be playing on equal terms.

But it wasn't as easy as he thought. The ball shot off the taut strings like a rocket, and it took him some time before he learned to adjust his shots, allowing the racquet to do most of the work. Then he began to volley crisply, tucking the balls away with renewed confidence.

After ten minutes, Frank seemed satisfied. "Good," he said, approaching the net, "now what about stop-volleys?"

Barry had no idea what he was talking about. "Stop-volleys?"

"Where you take all the speed off the ball. So it falls over the net and dies."

Barry shrugged. "Sure. No problem."

"Show me."

Frank moved back to the baseline, and sent a series of balls low over the net. But however hard Barry tried, he couldn't make them die. His volleys bounced as high as before, and Frank was able to return them without moving.

"Not as easy as you thought, eh?" Barry was annoyed to find Frank grinning at him.

He scuffed his feet on the shale. "It's the court. No one can make the ball die on this stuff."

"Yes they can."

"OK. *You* show *me*."

He walked away to the baseline, and Frank took his place at the net. He started driving for the corners, hard and low, but Frank cut off each ball with ease, slicing across them so that they looped slowly over the net, hardly bouncing at all.

Barry stared at him, impressed and curious. "Hey, how'd you do that?"

"It's all in the wrist. At the moment of impact, you flick it"—Frank demonstrated a quick, twisting movement—"like turning a key in a lock. Want a try?"

"Yeh." Barry resumed the net-position, and copied Frank's key-turning motion. The effect was miraculous. He found that he was able to take all the speed off the ball and send it spinning in a delicate little arc across the net, where it "died". Even Borg or McEnroe, if they had been standing on the baseline, couldn't have got it back.

"Right—that's it," said Frank, approaching the net again. "Useful shot to have in your locker, that—specially on grass."

"Grass?" Barry bounced his racquet-head on the net. "The only grass I seen is on the telly."

"Wimbledon?"

"Yeh."

"Like to play there, would you?"

Barry glanced at him, then looked quickly away. He hadn't told anyone about his secret ambition—the vision he often had just before he went to sleep, of Champion Grieves leaping the net on the Centre Court, with the cheers of fifteen thousand spectators ringing in his ears.

He wasn't sure how Frank would react to this. His impossible dream sounded so ridiculous, standing here in his shabby school gear. But what the hell? Every kid had fantasies about the great deeds he or she was going to do when they grew up. "I'd like to win the bleeding thing," he said softly. "All them foreigners holding up that cup every year—taking all that money out of the country. Somebody ought to do something about it."

To his surprise, Frank didn't laugh. He stood on the other side of the net, regarding Barry with thoughtful interest. "Somebody like you?" he asked gently.

"Me?" Barry banged the net again. "Fat chance."

"You never thought of making a living at tennis?"

"No."

"Why not?"

There were a thousand reasons why not, chief among which was his father. "Me Dad wouldn't wear it," he said resignedly. "He wants me to leave school soon as I've done me C.S.E. Get a job."

Frank smiled. "What's wrong with a job in sport?"

Barry could picture his father's face going purple at the suggestion. "That's not a proper job—not according to him. Maybe if a First Division Football Club was after me, he'd think different. But tennis—he says it's not for the likes of us."

"Suppose I had a chat with him after Lucy's lesson."

Barry stared at Frank, a faint hope beginning to burn like a small flame inside him. He didn't think there was much chance, but you never knew. If this bloke was supposed to be one of the best coaches in the country, he just might be able to swing it.

THREE

Life at home, thought Barry, as he sat in the passenger seat of Frank's car, hadn't been the same since his father had been made redundant. Home was a small, cramped semi—which seemed to have become even smaller now the old man was always there, looming, criticising, burning with resentment.

Mr Grieves was a proud, independent man who hated his enforced idleness. For over twenty years, he had been a porter at Covent Garden, but had lost his job when the market moved south of the river. Since then, he had worked as a lorry-driver, painter and decorator and builder's labourer; but each time, after a few weeks—or, at the most, a few months—he was given his cards. "Back on the scrap-heap," he would say to Barry's mother, handing her his final pay-packet.

He'd been out of work now for six months. Day by day his bitterness increased, expressing itself in outbursts of anger at both Barry and his mother—so that they had long since stopped feeling sorry for him and begun to resent his resentment. Hardly a day passed without a major row—usually over nothing.

The weekends were the worst. There was no escape from the brooding presence in the living-room sprawled in the armchair in front of the television. Sometimes Barry's mother wasn't there—she worked as an office cleaner to supplement his father's dole money, and took the occasional weekend job because of the overtime—so he and the old man were left alone. Barry knew his father hated the thought of his mother being the family breadwinner, and that it was this which prompted the eternal lectures about "making something of himself" and "learning a skill", but the depressing fact was that the old man had become a bore. They couldn't have the sort of conversations they used to have—about football, pop music, the Second World War—because the lines of communication had completely broken down.

So there was every chance that his father would blow his top when he heard what Frank had to say. But Barry had nothing to lose; and at least it would be Frank, not him, who would have to bear the brunt of the attack. It would make a change from their usual arguments, in which he and his mother would close ranks to defend each other from the old man's terrible tongue-lashings.

His mother was home, thank God, her reactions reassuringly predictable. She was always flustered by the arrival of an unexpected visitor, and Frank's appearance seemed to catch her completely off balance. Barry knew she was nervous from the way she kept chattering away, apologising for the state of the house and explaining at great length why it hadn't been dusted or cleaned since Sunday. She didn't ask questions; all she seemed concerned about was that this tall, track-suited stranger shouldn't get the impression the place was always in such a mess.

Frank listened to her long-winded excuses, smiling pleasantly. It was he who ought to apologise, he told her; he had no right to barge in like this, and if it was inconvenient, he could come back some other time. But he'd very much like a word with her and her husband about their son.

She glanced at Barry with a worried frown. "Why? Got himself into some sort of trouble has he?"

Frank laughed. "Not as far as I know. And I have a suggestion that might keep him out of it."

Barry could see that his mother didn't know what to make of this. Brushing a stray strand of hair from her eyes, she said, "Well, I'm sure you'd like a cup of tea. Why don't you go and have a chat to my husband while I put the kettle on?"

She disappeared into the kitchen, and Barry led the way into the living-room.

His father was sitting in his usual armchair, watching the early-evening news on the television. The volume was turned way up, and Barry had to shout to make himself heard.

"Dad? This is Frank Abbott. He wants to talk to you."

His father gave Frank a long, suspicious stare—then stood up, crossed over to the set and switched it off.

"What about?" he asked, looking at Barry.

"Me."

"You? Been up to your tricks again, eh?"

Marvellous, thought Barry; the way both his parents assumed, first off, that the appearance of a stranger meant he'd got himself into bother. From the way they carried on, he might've been the biggest villain in the manor. Frank must be wondering what he'd done to deserve such lack of trust.

But if Frank was wondering that, he showed no sign of it. He explained that he was a tennis coach, that he'd seen Barry practising in the park, and that he thought he showed exceptional promise. Had Mr Grieves ever considered tennis as a possible career for his son?

Barry's father listened, open-mouthed—occasionally glancing at Barry reproachfully, as if accusing him of hiding some dark, guilty secret.

When Frank had finished, there was a long, uncomfortable silence. Barry, sitting on the window-seat, bent down and picked some dried mud off his shoes to avoid his father's hostile glare.

"How come you was playing tennis in the park?"

Barry told him all about his secret morning sessions which he sandwiched in between his paper round and the beginning of school. His father seemed only slightly mollified to learn that no money was involved, and that Barry hadn't been playing truant. But he was still suspicious, obviously believing there must be some other reason why Barry had kept his visits to the park secret for eighteen months.

There was no time for explanations, however, because Mrs Grieves arrived with the tea-tray. Barry, relieved to have an ally present for what was likely to be a long and difficult battle, quickly brought her up to date, revealing that Frank thought he might be good enough to make a career in tennis.

His father contemptuously dismissed the idea. "Out of the question," he said firmly. "I'm not having Barry waste his time, messing about on tennis courts. A kid like him needs security."

Frank seemed not at all put out by this implied insult. "And where's he going to find that these days, Mr Grieves?" he asked, putting down his tea-cup. "With new technology eating up hundreds of jobs every week?"

Mr Grieves shrugged. "There's got to be something better than tennis."

"Tennis is part of the leisure industry. And with people having more and more time on their hands, it's going to be more and more important. I reckon Barry'd have as much security there as anywhere else."

Barry could see that his father didn't like the reference to people with time on their hands, but to his relief the old man chose to ignore it. "Suppose he doesn't make it?" he asked, leaning forward and tapping Frank on the knee. "He'd have nothing to fall back on, would he?"

"There's plenty of spin-off jobs," Frank told him. "He could even end up as a teaching Pro, like me."

"And how much do *you* earn, then?"

Frank smiled. "I'm not a good example."

"Why not?"

"Because I'm not in it for the money. If I was, I'd be a relatively rich man by now."

This was not the most tactful remark to someone out of work, and Barry knew it would annoy his father. Before he could reply, however, his mother intervened. She, at any rate, seemed to be giving Frank's suggestion serious consideration.

"But tennis—it's a summer game, right? What happens in the winter?"

Frank looked relieved that she had finally joined the conversation. "There's a demand for lessons as long as the courts are playable, Mrs Grieves. And even if there wasn't, a good Pro can make enough in the summer to cover him for the rest of the year."

Barry saw his mother and father exchange glances, and the flame of hope burned a little more brightly.

His mother turned back to Frank. "What are Barry's chances, Mr Abbott? Of making a decent living as a player?"

"Depends how much he puts into it—how hard he works. All I can say at the moment is that he shows promise."

"But so do thousands of other kids?"

"Right."

Barry thought Frank might have sounded a bit more encouraging, but his mother seemed to respect the fact that he wasn't making any extravagant claims. He was just beginning to think that things were going much better than he had expected, when his father returned to the fray—and the little flame flickered and almost died.

"No. I'm not having Barry swanning round the country playing games, while I'm on the dole and his mother has to go out scrubbing other people's floors. Soon as he leaves school, he's going to learn a trade."

"He *would* be learning a trade," said Frank earnestly. "Not the sort you're used to, maybe . . ."

"But it'd cost money. And we haven't enough for the necessities—let alone tennis lessons."

Barry heard the hurt and the despair in his father's voice, and, despite his disappointment, he felt sorry for him. He wished he could tell the old man that it didn't matter, but it was too late now. The gulf between them was too wide.

Frank rose, and stood with his back to the fireplace. "The lessons will be free," he said quietly.

Mr Grieves stared at him as if he couldn't believe his ears. "Eh?"

"There'll be no charge."

"What's in it for you, then?"

Frank looked thoughtful. "A coach gets his reputation from his brightest pupils. I earn my bread teaching wealthy businessmen and their wives—but it's the kids who really make my job worthwhile. And it's a long time since I came across a kid as special as Barry."

"Special?" Mrs Grieves, in the act of pouring herself another cup of tea, froze with astonishment. "You really think he's special?"

"I think he has a special talent. All he needs is to be taught how to use it."

Barry was amused to see both confusion and pride in his mother's face. "I never thought," she said slowly, "I mean—tennis. I never thought of it as a working-class game."

Frank's expression was grim. "No, Mrs Grieves. That's just the trouble."

"Trouble?"

"It's got the wrong image. People like you see all those women in fancy hats eating strawberries and cream at

Wimbledon and think 'That's not for us'. So lads like Barry slip through the net."

Barry waited anxiously for his mother and father to say something. But as both of them remained silent, he decided it was about time he stuck his oar in. He edged nervously forward, to stand by his father's chair. "Well, Dad?"

"Waste of time."

It sounded like the final verdict, but his mother came to his rescue. "What's he got to lose, Jack?"

"It's what *we've* got to lose I'm worried about. The wages Barry should be bringing in."

"Well, he's still got another couple of years at school," said Frank, "so you don't have to make a decision yet. Why don't I start giving him some lessons and see how we go?"

Barry watched his mother give his father an almost imperceptible nod. There was a long pause—then his father nodded back.

Barry's heart leaped. Perhaps his dream of jumping the net as Wimbledon champion wasn't so impossible after all!

*

This silver cloud, however, was not without its dark lining. When Barry entered the classroom the next day, Mr Miller told him curtly that the Headmaster wished to see him. From the grim expression on "Muscles'" face, reflected in those of his team-mates, he guessed what had happened; they'd lost the match, and they blamed him for the defeat.

Even the toughest boys were a little in awe of the Headmaster. Since his arrival two years ago, the change in the school had been dramatic. From a breeding ground for bullies and vandals, it had become a place where you could actually learn something; those who didn't want to learn no longer interfered with those who did, because the Headmaster, unlike his predecessor, believed in discipline. And the penalties for disruption were severe.

Barry tapped nervously on the door of the Headmaster's study, received a muffled "Come in", and entered.

The Headmaster, tall, grey-haired and distinguished-looking, was sitting at his desk. He gave no indication that he was aware of Barry's presence, but continued to cover a notepad with thin, spidery writing. Barry was just beginning to wonder if he had imagined the "Come in", when the Headmaster's voice made him jump.

"Sit down," he said, without looking up.

Barry sat down in the chair facing the desk and waited. At last, the Headmaster laid down his pen and stood up, grasping the edges of his gown as if he was preparing to address the whole school at assembly.

"Mr Miller tells me you refused to turn out for the Under-sixteen Cricket team yesterday. And that you left the playing fields before the end of the game without permission."

Barry felt extremely uncomfortable; the Headmaster's piercing blue eyes seemed to be boring into him like lasers. His sense of injustice, however, gave him the courage to speak up.

"School's supposed to finish at half-three, right?" he said defiantly.

"But cricket matches can't be fitted into a precise time-table—a boy of your experience must realise that. If everyone left at half-past-three, very few matches would reach a conclusion, would they?"

Barry stared down at his feet to avoid the blue lasers. To his relief, the Headmaster moved out of his line of vision.

"You know we lost the match yesterday."

"I sussed it from the way everyone looked at me."

"Can you blame them? We might not have lost if our star

batsman had been present. I'm afraid you've caused a good deal of resentment."

Barry remained silent, waiting for whatever punishment was coming to him. The Headmaster resumed his seat at the desk.

"A tennis lesson, Mr Miller said. Why couldn't you have postponed it?"

Barry found himself forced to look up. "The offer was for yesterday. If I'd turned it down, he might've thought I wasn't interested."

"Who's 'he'?"

"This Pro I met down at the park. Reckons I've got potential."

The Headmaster leaned forward, folding his hands on the desk. "But you can play tennis during the holidays. It's not part of the school curriculum."

"Why not?"

"Because we don't have the facilities. And—more important—because it's not a team game."

This seemed a very poor reason, and Barry felt he had to make a protest: "What's so special about team games?"

"They're a good preparation for adult life. Most jobs involve teamwork of some kind—so we have to learn to pull together."

"I don't fancy being part of a team."

The Headmaster smiled, as if this wasn't the first time he'd heard such a remark. " 'No man is an island', Barry," he said quietly. "Chap called John Donne wrote that—and he was right. We're all part of the human race, and whether we like it or not we have to rely on other people."

"What for?"

"Just about everything. To care for us. Protect us. Love us."

Barry wasn't going to let him get away with that. "And drop catches?" he asked slyly.

"What?"

"Last cricket match I played in, there was three dropped catches. That's what you get when you rely on people . . ."

The Headmaster's tone turned icy. "You must try to be a little more charitable, Barry. Not everyone is blessed with your athletic prowess."

"That's why I'd sooner rely on me'self. I know where I am then."

"And what about the school?"

Barry felt the lasers boring into him again. "What about it?"

"You don't feel you owe us anything?"

"No."

The Headmaster stared at him with distaste. "Then there's no more to be said."

"I can go?"

"You can go. I just hope that one day you'll learn to give as well as take."

*

For the rest of the morning, Barry found it hard to concentrate. The Headmaster obviously agreed with Mr Miller that he had been extremely selfish, but he still didn't see why he should feel guilty. Surely he should be allowed to do as he liked with his free time? He hadn't broken any school rules, so what were they on about? He felt he'd been treated very unfairly.

But worse was to come. He was on his way home after school, walking down the narrow path that ran round the edge of the allotments, when Greg and Dennis stepped out of the undergrowth, barring his way.

He stopped abruptly. This is it, he thought—I'm in for a

good thumping. He knew he could outrun them, but that was out of the question. To show them he was afraid would give them something to crow about, and in any case he would only be postponing the day of reckoning. Better to take what was coming to him here and now.

He moved slowly forward to within a few feet of them, waiting for them to speak their piece.

"Hi, Barry," said Greg pleasantly, "heard about the match, did you?"

"Yeh. Tough."

"They wasn't much," said Dennis. "If you'd 've played, we'd 've walked it."

Barry stared at him, tensing himself for the inevitable punch-up. "Come on, Dennis. I could've been out first ball."

Greg began his usual tactic of moving round behind him. "Well we'll never know, will we? On account of you wasn't there."

"On account of you had something better to do," added Dennis.

Barry stood his ground; this time, he wasn't going to give Greg the satisfaction of turning round. Besides, whichever way he turned, there would always be one of them behind him.

"The lads feel you let 'em down." Greg's voice was now tinged with menace. "There was a vote to give you a bit of a spanking, but Dennis and me—we talked 'em out of it."

"Nice one," said Barry. "Ta."

Dennis moved a step forward, his arms hanging loosely by his sides. "We said it wasn't worth getting heavy. Long as you promise to show up for the rest of the matches."

"I can't promise that. I want to do me own thing for the rest of the term."

"It's not what *you* want, Barry. It's what *we* want."

"Why?"

" 'Cos there are ten of us, and only one of you—that's why."

Barry decided the time had come to give them the excuse they were waiting for. "Oh, shove off," he said irritably, giving Dennis a light push in the chest.

Caught momentarily off balance, Dennis staggered backwards, leaving the way clear. Barry started to walk away, but when he heard footsteps behind him, turned quickly—just in time to dodge a blow from Greg that would have knocked him cold if it had connected.

He punched Greg hard in the stomach, but had no chance to follow up his attack. Dennis launched himself at Barry's legs, bringing him crashing to the ground in a rugby tackle.

He tried to scramble to his feet, but Greg kicked him in the ribs, propelling him sideways on to the grass at the edge of the path. From then on, he just had to defend himself as best he could. His assailants piled on top of him, raining down blows and kicks. He covered his face with his hands and rolled himself into a tight little ball to leave as small a target as possible, but it was no use; for every blow he parried, two got through his protective screen.

At first, the pain was excruciating. But gradually, as his brain began to swim, he felt the blows less and less. It didn't seem to matter how many times they hit him; they couldn't hurt him any more.

He was just beginning to lose consciousness when the blows suddenly stopped. He opened a badly bruised eye and saw them standing over him, panting heavily. They nodded to each other, as if satisfied with their handiwork, and moved off down the path.

So that's over, he thought grimly. They'd had their fun; now he was entitled to his.

*

He had no idea how he got home. The next thing he remembered was his mother's horrified expression as, standing behind the ironing-board in the living-room, she looked up and saw his face.

"Barry!" She remained frozen with shock for a moment, holding the iron in mid-air. Then she set it down carefully, crossed over to him and held him at arm's length, turning his head to inspect his cuts and bruises.

"What happened?" she demanded, with a worried frown.

"I wouldn't play for 'em now if they killed me," Barry grunted through thick and battered lips.

"Play for who?"

"The school. Bleeding sods ..."

She stared searchingly into his half-closed eyes. "Who was it, love? Who thumped you?"

Barry broke away from her and slumped wearily into a chair. "Forget it."

"How can I forget it? I'm the one who has to wash your clothes—mend the tears so you don't look like a scarecrow."

He looked up at her blearily. All he wanted to do was go upstairs and lie down, but he realised he wasn't the only one who would suffer as a result of the fight. "I know, Mum—I'm sorry. But it wasn't my fault—honest."

She seemed to accept that she wasn't going to get any more information out of him. She held out her hand. "Let's have them trousers, then. I'll put 'em in to soak."

As he stood up and started to take off his trousers, she asked: "What was all that about not playing for the school?"

"I'm not—not ever again. *I'm* the one I'm going to play for. And if I win, it'll be for me, get it? Not the school, not the country ..."

"Not even me?"

He turned to hand her his trousers, and found to his

surprise that she was smiling at him. "You?" he asked, puzzled by her sudden change of mood.

"Well, be fair. If I look after your clothes, I got a right to expect something in return, haven't I?"

He grinned at her—a painful exercise as it widened the splits in his lips. "OK, Mum," he agreed, "I'll play for us."

"Ta." She turned and disappeared through the door.

Barry was just about to collapse back into the chair, when he noticed the photo of Bjorn Borg that he'd cut out of a newspaper and slipped into the empty picture-frame on the sideboard.

He crossed over and picked it up. Borg was caught in mid-air as he jumped the net, yet another Wimbledon victory under his belt. If only he wasn't Swedish, thought Barry; if only he himself was five years older . . .

He put the picture-frame down, turned and saw the ironing-board. Forcing his aching limbs to obey him, he took a running jump and soared over it, shirt-tails flapping and arms outstretched in triumph.

FOUR

They left him alone after that. Mr Miller, having heard about the attack, and obviously feeling guilty for having provoked it, tried several times to make amends—but Barry rejected his peace offers. He was happy with things as they were; "Muscles" and the cricketers on one side of the fence, and himself on the other. They could go on dropping catches off each other, and he could get on with his life.

And life now revolved around his daily lessons with Frank. They became the focus of all his attention, gave his humdrum routine a new purpose and meaning. For five hours a week, he forgot about school, about his father, about his paper round—and concentrated on the only thing he really cared about.

Under Frank's careful tuition, he improved rapidly. His ground-shots became grooved, so that he made less and less unforced errors; and he started to learn about match-play, to resist the temptation to belt the cover off the ball and wait for right opening before advancing to the net.

One thing niggled him, however. He never forgot he was taking Frank's charity—borrowing his racquets, using his balls. And it was Frank who paid the court fees which, even in the park, still amounted to two pounds fifty a week.

Barry was determined to get his own racquet, to pay his own way as soon as possible. So when his father told him of a mate of his—a wholesale greengrocer—who needed someone to hump crates for an hour every morning, he took it. Now he could really start to save up for his own tennis gear.

But the new job took its toll. It meant having to get up at five-thirty every morning, load crates on to lorries for an hour—and then set off on his paper round. He began to feel very tired, and by four o'clock—the time of his lesson—he found it difficult to raise much of a gallop.

He tried to hide his weariness from Frank, but one Friday, after a particularly gruelling rally, his knees suddenly gave way—and he collapsed to the ground, exhausted.

Frank moved round the net, helped him to his feet and sat him on the bench. "You OK?" he asked anxiously.

Barry sat with his head between his knees. "Yeh. I'm just—a bit—knackered."

"Knackered? After half an hour? Suppose this was Wimbledon?"

"If it was Wimbledon, I wouldn't be doing me paper round, would I?"

Frank stood looking down at him, frowning with concern. "What time did you get up this morning?"

Here it comes, thought Barry, he's going to start getting heavy. "Dunno," he said evasively.

"Come on, Barry—you must've set the alarm. What time?"

There was obviously no way he could keep his new job secret any longer. "Half-five."

Frank looked horrified. "Half-past *five*? Nobody starts a paper round that early!"

"Well, I got this other job, haven't I?"

"What job?"

"Shiftin' boxes of fruit."

"And then you do your paper round?"

Barry shrugged. "I can do with the extra readies."

Frank contemplated him in silence for a moment. Then he shook his head. "It's too much, Barry. You're burning yourself out."

"I'll be OK. Soon as I get me wind back."

"No. It's affecting your stamina. You can't go on like this."

"I got to," said Barry desperately, "I earn one-fifty a day at the greengrocer's—that's seven-fifty a week. If I went back to Dad and said I was chucking it in because it was putting the mockers on me tennis, he'd go spare. And it's not just that . . ."

"What d'you mean?"

"I can't go on borrowing your gear, can I? Taking your hand-outs? Living on your charity?"

Frank grabbed his arm, swinging him round so that they sat face to face. "It's nothing to do with charity, Barry. As far as I'm concerned, you're an investment. Maybe you'll pay off, maybe you won't—but it's a chance I'm prepared to take."

"Well, I don't fancy it," Barry told him, "and neither does Dad. We don't like not being able to chip in."

They stood up and walked slowly across to the gate. Frank paused, his hand on the latch. "Suppose I got you some sponsorship?"

Barry stared at him. "Eh?"

"Someone to pay your expenses. Take the financial pressure off. It's a little early—but I might be able to fix it."

"You're joking. I mean—who's going to sponsor some kid they never even heard of?"

Frank smiled. "They've heard of me."

"And they'll take your word?"

"Maybe. But you'll stand a better chance if I could get you into the Club."

Barry thought that Frank was out of his mind. Major Houghton had obviously taken an instant dislike to him, believing he was a potential thief—which meant he had as much chance of being accepted as a member as Jason had of making the school cricket team. But he said nothing. If Frank thought it was worth a try, there was no point in arguing.

As they drove up the hill in Frank's car, Barry found himself becoming nervous. He began to realise that a lot depended on getting into a club. Anyone thinking of sponsoring him would be likely to take him much more seriously, and not think of him as some snotty kid for whom tennis was just a passing phase. And once he had a sponsor, then even more people—perhaps really important people—would start to take him seriously ...

Major Houghton was standing by the courts, watching four elderly ladies patting the ball gently backwards and forwards across the net. Barry sat on one of the benches, once again conscious of the shabbiness of his appearance, as Frank made his pitch.

He was within earshot, and though he tried to pretend he wasn't eavesdropping, overheard the whole conversation.

The Major's first reaction was depressingly negative. "I'm afraid it's out of the question," he said firmly. "We've a six-month waiting-list."

"Not for the free places, Major." Frank seemed to know as much about the Club as the Secretary. "There's still a couple of vacancies."

"But we don't *have* to fill them—it's at the discretion of the Committee. And they're not too keen to take in any more young tearaways after that Poskett business."

This was the second time the Major had mentioned someone called Poskett, and Barry wondered who he was and what he had done. He didn't like the reference to "young tearaways", but he wasn't surprised; men like Major Houghton always thought of kids like him as trouble-makers.

He was glad to hear Frank spring to his defence. "Barry's not a tearaway," he said quietly.

The Major glanced in Barry's direction. "Guarantee that, can you?"

"I can guarantee that if you don't snap him up, someone else will."

"Good as that, is he?"

Frank lowered his voice, but Barry could still hear him clearly; and what he heard made him tingle with pleasure. "There's no one in this Club who could take a set off him. And I've hardly started working on him yet."

The Major looked impressed. "You'll take the responsibility if there's any trouble?"

"Yes," said Frank, without hesitation.

"You realise what that means, Frank? Your position at this Club could be at stake."

"I said I'd take the responsibility, Major."

"Very well."

The two men moved over towards Barry, who jumped up from the bench as they approached. But the Major told him to "sit down, young feller," and he resumed his seat.

"Mr Abbott tells me you're an exciting prospect." The Major had taken out a tobacco-pouch and was filling a pipe. "Says we ought to snap you up."

Barry glanced at Frank and grinned. He'd had no idea the coach thought so much of him.

The Major put his foot up on the bench, pressing down the strands of tobacco with his thumb. "Point is this. We do have a few free places for promising youngsters—but in return, we expect them to behave themselves. Understood?"

"Yeh," said Barry, trying not to let his excitement show too much.

"I'm sorry I jumped to the wrong conclusion when I found you in the changing room that day. But we caught a boy stealing some months ago, so I was naturally suspicious."

The old soldier didn't seem so bad after all, and Barry eagerly accepted the olive branch. "That's OK," he said magnanimously.

"Now we have strict rules at this Club," the Major went on. "After six o'clock, juniors must vacate their courts if they're required by an adult member. And whites must be worn at all times . . ."

Barry's face fell. He couldn't even afford his own racquet yet, let alone the full gear. It seemed an insuperable obstacle, and he was about to explain to the Major why he couldn't become a member, even for free—when he saw Frank give a little shake of his head. So he remained silent, wondering how many weeks it would take him to save up enough money for a complete outfit.

Back in the car park, he told Frank of his problem. But the coach seemed unconcerned. "Don't worry. I'll help you out," he said airily, as if Barry was making a fuss over nothing.

He still didn't seem to understand that to accept free lessons from him was one thing, but to allow him to pay for the proper gear was quite another. "I don't need your help," Barry told him fiercely. "Just tell me how much it'll come to."

Frank thought for a moment. "Maybe fifty quid."

"And the racquet?"

"Another forty."

Ninety quid! Barry did a few rapid calculations. He had nearly thirty pounds saved up, and at his present rate of income, he could pay off the rest in about two months.

But when he suggested this, Frank shook his head firmly.

"I want you to give up your second job, Barry. If you insist on paying me back, I'd rather wait longer for the money than have you come to the lessons too tired to do yourself justice."

Barry nodded. "OK. Just as long as I *do* pay you back."

They climbed into the car, but before Frank could start the engine Lucy appeared on a bicycle, her racquet strapped to the handlebars. She freewheeled up to them and peered in through the window.

"Hello, Frank," she said, ignoring Barry, "I've been meaning to ask you. Have you got the entry forms for the County Under-sixteens yet?"

"Not yet. If they haven't arrived by tomorrow, I'll give 'em a ring."

"Thanks."

Lucy turned her cycle away from the car, but Frank called her back. "Oh Lucy!" Her face reappeared at the window. "I've got a teach-in down in Sussex tomorrow, so I'm afraid I shall have to cancel all my lessons. Why don't you work out with Barry after school?"

Barry opened his mouth to protest that he'd much rather practise by himself, but thought better of it. Perhaps Frank wanted him to help this girl, give her a few tips about what she was doing wrong. And as the coach was giving up five hours a week to help him improve *his* game, the least he could do was to pass on some of the knowledge he had gained.

Lucy, however, seemed to like the idea of a shared work-out even less than he did. "OK," she said, with a marked lack of enthusiasm. "What time can you be here?"

" 'Round four," he told her.

"Right. See you then." She pedalled off in the direction of the courts.

It was only then that Barry remembered that his big

problem was still unsolved. "What about me whites?" he asked plaintively.

Frank started the engine. "I'm taking you shopping," he said, reversing out of the parking bay. "By tomorrow, you'll be the smartest kid in the Club."

*

Barry's father eyed the new gear suspiciously. "How much did this lot cost, then?"

Barry had laid it all out on the dining table: four shirts, six pairs of socks, two pairs of shorts, a pair of tennis shoes . . . and the new racquet, carefully selected by Frank for its weight and balance.

He swallowed hard; this was going to be very tricky. "Nearly a hundred quid, Dad," he said, trying to make it sound like fifty pence.

"A hundred quid!" His father stared at him, open-mouthed. "You must be out of your mind."

"I got to have the new gear. It's the Club rules."

"Club rules my Aunt Fanny! You know how long your mother has to work to make a hundred quid? Fifty hours."

"I don't mind, Jack," Barry's mother came bustling in with the tea-tray. "It's in a good cause."

"Good cause? You mean you don't mind scrubbing floors so he can go poncing around on a tennis court dressed like a tailor's dummy?"

"It's my money," said Barry defiantly. "Or it will be. I'm going to pay Frank back—every penny."

"So it's 'Frank' now, is it?" His father's face was becoming red with anger. "I suppose it was him put you up to buying all this rubbish."

"All he did was introduce me to the Club so I'd stand a better chance of finding a sponsor. Only the geezer there says I've got to have whites."

"I got you that job down the greengrocer's so you could earn your keep, not throw it away on fancy clobber like this."

Barry's mother handed him a cup of tea. "Be fair, Jack. You said he could go on with his tennis . . ."

"Long as it didn't cost me. That's what I said—right, Barry?"

Barry sighed. "It's not costing you, Dad. I'm the one that's paying for it."

"Which means your mother has to pay for your keep!"

"He's only fourteen, Jack." Mrs Grieves picked up one of the shirts and tested the quality of the material between forefinger and thumb. "We *should* be paying for his keep."

Barry tried to pour oil on troubled waters. "All I need's a bit of time . . . till I can get some sponsorship."

"Sponsorship?" His father snorted contemptuously. "Who's going to sponsor *you*, eh?"

"Dunno. But Frank reckons he can fix it."

"It's a con—that's what it is—a bleeding con! I don't know what this precious Frank of yours is up to, but you're not wasting another penny on tennis gear. You hear me? From now on, you hand over all your wages to me and your mother. If there's a quid or two left over, *we'll* decide what to spend it on." He turned and stalked out of the room.

Barry stood staring disconsolately down at his new racquet. The tremendous excitement he had felt when he and Frank had bought it was now replaced by a sense of guilt. With money so tight, perhaps it was selfish of him to spend so much on himself.

His mother approached and put a comforting arm round his shoulder. "Don't worry, love. Your father's not himself at the moment."

"I couldn't go on borrowing Frank's racquets, Mum—it wasn't right. I had to have one of me own."

"Course you did, love. I understand."

"I wish Dad did." Barry broke away from her and wandered over to the mantelpiece. "And there's something else. Frank wants me to give up the greengrocer's job. Says it's making me too knackered."

"Yes. I think he's right."

Barry whirled round in surprise. "You do? But what about Dad? What'll he say if I pack it in?"

His mother smiled. "Leave it to me. I'll work on him."

*

When he arrived at the Club the next day, he found Lucy already on court, practising her service.

She grinned when she saw him. "New gear, eh? Very smart."

He scowled at her. "Just don't go on about it, OK?"

"OK."

He took the cover off his new racquet. "So. What d'you want to do?"

For some reason, the question seemed to annoy her. "What d'you mean—what do *I* want to do?"

"There's nothing special you want to work on? Backhand, volley, smash? Maybe I could give you a few tips."

She frowned. "I take my lessons from Frank, Clever-Clogs. We're supposed to work out *together*."

Barry couldn't understand why she was being so prickly, but he wanted to make it clear that as far as he was concerned the whole thing was a waste of time. "Suit yourself," he said with studied indifference. "Just trying to be useful. I mean, *I'm* not going to get much of a work-out, am I?"

She put her hands on her hips and stared at him, her mouth tight and grim. "I'm not good enough for you, eh?"

"Nothing personal. But it stands to reason, dunnit? Birds can't hit as hard as fellers, they can't run as fast, their reactions are slower . . ."

"In other words, we're just inferior?"

"On a tennis court—yeh."

She produced a stick of gum and started to unwrap it. "Tell you what—I'll take the net and you try and pass me. Show me how superior you are."

Barry shrugged. If she wanted him to make a fool of her, he was quite prepared to do it. Some of these birds seemed to think they could compete with boys on equal terms, and he was glad of the chance to teach this one a lesson. Just because she spoke like the Queen, she thought she was the cat's whiskers. Well, he'd show her.

He moved to the baseline, and Lucy took the net position. At first he didn't try very hard, confident that even at half-pace his passing shots would be too good for her. But she cut them off with ease, volleying cross-court and down the lines with surprising power.

Gradually, he increased the pace—but still she picked off the balls, scuttling from side to side like a little terrier.

"Not bad," he said grudgingly.

"You mean—for a bird?"

"Yeh."

She smiled. "You want to take the net?"

They changed places, and now it was Barry's turn to dominate the court. Her ground-shots were low and accurate, but gave him no trouble; compared with Frank's screaming drives, these were a doddle.

He began to tease her, increasing the angle of his volleys so that she had to run wider and wider in order to retrieve them. Her face became redder and redder, but she never gave up, flinging herself at each ball with grim determination.

After one particularly long and gruelling rally, he collapsed with laughter. He didn't mean to take the mickey—in fact, he had begun to feel a reluctant admiration for her—but she took it the wrong way.

She regarded him balefully, hands on hips and shoulders heaving. "What's the matter?"

He grinned at her. "Nothing."

"Come on, Barry—what's so funny?"

"You. Scuttling around like a little insect . . ."

"Right. That's it." She marched to the side of the court, threw her racquet into her tennis bag.

Barry watched her, puzzled. "Eh?"

"That's it. I'm off."

"Why? What did I say?"

She whirled round on him furiously. "I'm not going to waste my time with a conceited little chauvinist who thinks girls are beneath him. I'd rather practise against a wall."

Barry, surprised and disconcerted by this outburst, tried to make amends. "I couldn't help laughing. You looked so funny."

"I don't care how I look. All I care about is tennis—and if you can't take it seriously, I'll find someone who will." She picked up her bag and walked off towards the gate.

Barry wasn't going to let her get away without letting her know how *he* felt. He called after her. "That's just an excuse, innit?"

She turned, looking startled. "What?"

"I saw you clocking me before I got this new gear. You thought, what a common little kid, I don't fancy being seen on the same court with him. But you couldn't say nothing, could you—not in front of Frank? So you was just waiting for an excuse to get out of it."

"I was not. I just don't like your manners, that's all."

"Manners? Blimey, I've met some toffee-nosed birds in my

time, but you're a right fancy-knickers. It's you who thinks everyone's beneath her."

She stood blinking at him for a long moment. Then, with a choked sob, she turned and ran off down the path towards the car park.

Barry watched her go with satisfaction. Who did she think she was, calling him a conceited little chauvinist? Well, now she knew what *he* thought of *her*. And it looked as though there'd be tears before bedtime.

FIVE

In fact, there were tears in the car park. As soon as Lucy was out of sight of the courts, she dropped her bag and buried her head in her hands, weeping silently.

That snotty little kid! He obviously thought he was God's gift to tennis, and no one else had a right to be on the court. It was so unfair, she thought bitterly, to call her toffee-nosed. She couldn't care less what he looked like, how he talked; as she'd told him, the only thing she cared about was tennis.

Of course, he couldn't possibly know how much she hated being told she was like an insect: how it reminded her of the nickname her sister Wendy had given her—a real put-down that made her seethe with anger. Now she came to think of it, Barry and Wendy had a lot in common; they both thought they were the greatest things since sliced bread.

She wiped her eyes on her tennis-shirt, picked up her bag and strapped it to the carrier on the back of her bike. It had been a really grotty day, she thought as she cycled out of the car-park. First of all she'd had yet another row with Wendy at breakfast, then the afternoon practice period at school had turned into the usual farce . . .

Miss Brotherton, the games mistress, hadn't the faintest interest in tennis, and had no idea how to teach it. As an ex-international, she was a whiz at netball and hockey; but when it came to tennis, she just couldn't be bothered. She let the girls make up their own games, which usually degenerated into gossip-sessions.

The trouble was, as Miss Brotherton had told Lucy that afternoon, there was no one at the school who could even give her a game. Bored to tears, Lucy had challenged Celia, the second-best girl, to a match in which she offered to play left-handed. They had agreed to put fifty pence on it, to give themselves something to fight for.

Lucy was leading five–three when Miss Brotherton interrupted them to ask what they were doing. When Celia explained they were playing for money, Miss Brotherton told them not to waste their time.

"It's a waste of time playing her right-handed, Miss Brotherton," Lucy had protested, "she can hardly get the ball back."

"So why don't you give her some practice? Maybe she'll improve."

"I'm the one who needs practice."

"Well I'm afraid there's nothing I can do about that," said Miss Brotherton briskly. "The school is unable to provide another girl of your exalted standard."

"But I'm supposed to be learning, not teaching. Couldn't I go early? At least there's a practice-wall at the Club."

Celia had supported her eagerly. "Oh, do let her go, please. You'll save me fifty pence."

And Miss Brotherton had reluctantly agreed. Despite losing the chance to make fifty pence, Lucy was delighted not to have to stay for the rest of the period; she was looking forward to testing herself against the kid Frank had just taken on, and she was determined to give a good account of herself. Now she had an extra half-hour in which to get herself into shape before he arrived.

She might just as well not have bothered, because he'd turned out to be such a pain. It was a pity, because from what she'd seen, he looked pretty useful. But she wasn't going to be humiliated by a cocky little brat who could hardly see over the net. She suffered enough humiliation at home.

She changed gear as she reached the bottom of the hill and stood up on the pedals. This was the hard bit—it took her a good six minutes from the bottom to the top—but she told herself it was part of her training, it strengthened the leg muscles.

Today, however, the six minutes' torture was particularly painful. The sense of gloom that had stayed with her ever since her row with Barry seemed to weigh her down. She was always having rows, she thought despondently—with Wendy, with her mother, with Miss Brotherton. And now this kid. The only person she never had rows with was her father—but he was so often away at meetings and conferences he was almost a stranger. She remembered when he had first shown her round the house at the top of the hill, with its glorious views over the rooftops of London, she had felt so close to him then. And she had looked forward so much to living there—the rooms had seemed so airy and spacious. Now, she just felt isolated.

She had no close friends at school. There was no one who shared her interest in tennis, and she knew the other girls looked on her as an oddball for her single-minded dedication to the game. Wendy certainly shared that view and her mother, though she occasionally came to see her play, made little effort to hide her boredom. None of them seemed to understand why tennis was so important to her—that it was the one thing she could do better than anyone else, that made her stand out in a crowd.

It was with relief that she freewheeled into the garage and dismounted. She suddenly realised she was hungry, and dashed into the kitchen to make herself a sandwich.

Wendy was sitting at the kitchen table, staring at her reflection in a hand-mirror.

"Where's Mum?" asked Lucy.

"Having her hair done. She left you some sandwiches."

Lucy collected the cellophane-wrapped plate from the sideboard, took a bottle of milk out of the fridge, and sat down opposite her sister. Wendy continued to inspect her face, turning it from side to side and pouting her lips like a fashion-model.

God, she's beautiful, thought Lucy, wolfing down the sandwiches. With her looks, she was bound to become a film star—even if she turned out to have no talent as an actress. It was so unfair; a stranger, seeing them together, would never believe they were sisters.

Wendy was eighteen—three years older than Lucy—and had just started her second year at drama school. Physically, they were as different as chalk from cheese; whereas Lucy was small and compact, Wendy was tall and willowy. Lucy had hoped that as they grew older they would grow more alike, but the hope had gradually died. She knew now that she would never have her sister's figure.

Wendy put down her mirror and stared at Lucy's tennis clothes. "Been at it again, I see."

"At what?"

"Honestly, Beetle, haven't you got any other interests in life? I mean—hitting a ball backwards and forwards across a net. It's pathetic!"

Here we go again, thought Lucy, another row. "Not as pathetic as admiring yourself in a mirror all day," she said sourly.

"I wasn't admiring myself—I was getting to know my face. Mr Hawkins says all actors should get to know their faces *intimately*."

"Who's Mr Hawkins?"

"He takes us for make-up. I think he's got a crush on me."

Wendy thought that about every man. "That's what you said about the other teacher," said Lucy, "the one who directed you in that Shakespeare thing."

"And I was right. He made a pass at me at the first-night party."

"You never told me."

"There's a lot of things I never tell you, Beetle dear. You're much too young."

Lucy bristled. "I'm only three years younger than you. And Mum told you to stop calling me that."

"Beetle?" Wendy smiled. "I can't think why you make such a fuss about it. It's a term of endearment."

"No, it isn't. You're trying to put me down."

"Rubbish. Beetles are sweet little things—scuttling about—always on the go. Just like you on a tennis court. Not particularly graceful, I admit, but such energy!"

Lucy stood up angrily. "Oh, shut up!"

"Finished already?" Wendy raised her plucked eyebrows in mock amazement. "You oughtn't to gobble up your food like that, specially after cycling up that hill. You'll give yourself indigestion."

"How would you know? The only exercise you ever take is painting your fingernails." Lucy flounced out of the kitchen, pleased that for once she'd had the last word.

She had a long, relaxing bath, which she refused to cut short when Wendy banged on the door and told her to hurry up. This led to another row when she finally came out, and to Wendy losing her temper. Lucy kept her own, and felt that she came out of the argument with much more dignity—so that by the time she came downstairs her depression had completely disappeared.

Her mother was cooking the dinner, her hair noticeably blonder since her visit to the hairdresser's.

"Hello, darling," she said, when she saw Lucy. "Have a nice game?"

"No." Lucy helped herself to a handful of grated cheese.

"I thought you told me you were playing someone rather good. Some boy Frank introduced you to."

"That's right."

"And he wasn't up to your standard? How disappointing." Her mother bent down and pulled a sizzling leg of lamb out of the oven, prodding it with a fork. "Lay the table, will you, dear? Daddy won't be home for dinner, so we'll eat in here tonight."

Lucy frowned. "Why can't Wendy do it?"

"She's learning her lines. She has to know the whole of the first act by tomorrow."

"Oh, for heaven's sake, Mummy . . ." Wendy always had some excuse. "It's only a drama school production! Anyone'd think she was opening in the West End."

Her mother slid the leg of lamb back in the oven. "It's her first leading part. And a couple of well-known critics have promised to come."

"I still don't see why she can't pull her weight around here," said Lucy crossly, "I have to do everything."

"Don't be silly, dear. This play's important for Wendy's career. So we must do all we can to help her."

Lucy opened the cutlery drawer and started to lay the table. "Well, it'll be her turn in a couple of weeks."

"Why?"

"It's the County Under-sixteens. And that's important for *my* career."

"Oh yes," said her mother vaguely, "I'd forgotten."

"You *are* coming?"

"Of course. When does it start?"

"A week on Monday. The fifteenth."

"I'll put it in my diary."

Her mother wiped her hands on a tea-cloth, opened her bag, which was lying on the sideboard, and took out her diary. She leafed through the pages—then frowned. "Oh dear."

"What?"

"That's Wendy's opening night." It would be, thought Lucy bitterly. "Never mind. I'll pop down on Tuesday or Wednesday. You'll still be playing, won't you?"

"If I'm not knocked out. What about Daddy?"

Her mother consulted her diary again. "I'm afraid he'll be up to his eyes that week. He has his Annual General Meeting on the Thursday."

Lucy nodded; if it hadn't been a meeting, it would have been a conference. "He'll be able to make Wendy's first night though?" she asked, trying to keep the hurt out of her voice.

"Oh yes. He wouldn't want to miss that."

"No. None of us would want to miss that."

Her mother glanced at her sharply, opened her mouth to say something, then appeared to have second thoughts. She turned away to the sink and started to top and tail some French beans.

*

When Barry arrived home, he looked into the living-room, saw his father alone in front of the television, and moved on towards the stairs. He didn't think the old man had heard him, but he was wrong.

"Barry?"

Reluctantly, he went back and stood nervously twiddling his racquet.

His father stared up at him expressionlessly. "Fancy yourself, do you? In that posh gear?"

"It's not posh, Dad. Just new."

"You know what you're doing? You're stepping out of your class—and that's asking for trouble."

"Why?"

" 'Cos they won't accept you, that's why."

Barry shrugged. "They already have."

"No, they haven't. All they've done is let you play in their yard. Made you wear their uniform. But they won't socialise with you—you'll see."

There was something in his father's tone that made Barry take him seriously. "I don't want to socialise with them," he said. "I just want to play tennis."

"You got to have someone to play *with*, haven't you? And they won't want to know."

"Why not?"

" 'Cos it's a snobby game—always has been. Take my advice and stick to your own. That way, you won't get hurt."

It seemed to be a genuine warning, offered for his own good, and Barry didn't want to sound ungrateful. But the old man was living in the past. "You're out of date, Dad," he told him gently, "Frank says there's more and more working-class lads. . . ."

"And whatever Frank says goes, does it? Half a dozen free lessons, and suddenly he's God?"

"Well, he knows more about it than you." This hadn't come out the way he meant it, and he tried to make amends. "I mean—when was the last time you was at a tennis club?"

"I don't have to go there to know the sort of people they are."

Yes, you do, thought Barry. And it might not be such a bad idea. "Why don't you come down tomorrow?" he suggested. "Have a look round?"

His father looked startled. "Me?"

"Yeh. About time you saw me play, innit?"

*

He didn't raise the subject again, and he had no idea whether the seed he had planted would take root. The odds were against it, he thought, as he arrived at the Club the next day; if the old man thought, as he obviously did, that Barry was wasting his time playing tennis, then he'd be bound to think he'd be wasting his own time watching him.

In the pavilion, he found Major Houghton behind the bar, helping himself to a whisky. Feeling thirsty, he walked up to the counter, and slapped down twenty pence.

"'Lo, Major. How about a lemonade?"

Houghton shook his head. "Sorry. The bar doesn't open till six."

"Looks like it's open for you."

"I'm the Club Secretary. That entitles me to certain privileges . . ."

Barry grinned. "Like having a booze-up on the house?"

"I beg your pardon?" The Major stared at him coldly.

"You just help yourself whenever you feel like it, right?"

He had meant this as a joke, but it didn't seem to go down too well. "No, I do not," said the Major grimly. "And you'd better watch your tongue, young man."

Barry held up his hands. "No offence, Major. Got yourself a cushy number here though, haven't you? Your own private pub."

He picked up his money and disappeared into the changing room. He realised he'd been very stupid to take the mickey out of Houghton; he couldn't afford to make so powerful an enemy. But it seemed absurd that the Club Secretary could have a whisky, and he couldn't even have a lemonade. He reckoned he was entitled to his bit of fun.

By the time he'd changed, there was only one court left unoccupied—the one nearest the pavilion. There was no sign of Frank, so Barry collected a box of old balls from the shelf just inside the pavilion door, took them on court and began practising his service.

He set himself a routine, serving six times from one end into the left-hand court, then six times from the other into the right. There were two elderly men next to him, engaged in a life-and-death struggle in which the rallies seemed to go on for ever. Barry watched them with amusement as he changed ends; both were sweating profusely, both looked ready to drop, but they were obviously willing to die rather than lose a point. He felt a grudging admiration for them; they weren't much good, and no one else cared who won and who lost. But *they* cared. It was a matter of pride, of fighting their advancing years. He hoped he still had as much competitive spirit when he was their age.

"Grieves?" He turned and saw Major Houghton standing by the wire. "This court's reserved."

Terrific, thought Barry, when Frank arrived, they'd have to schlep all the way to the park.

He walked over to the Major. "Reserved? Who for?"

"Ladies doubles. They play here every week at this time."

"Well they're not here yet, are they?"

"I'm just warning you. You'll have to come off as soon as they arrive.'

Barry felt sure the Major was winding him up because of their little confrontation in the pavilion. "Where'm I supposed to play then?"

"If you want to be sure of a court, you'll have to play earlier."

"Why can't the old bats play earlier? They don't have to go to school."

The Major seemed to make a great effort to control his temper. "The old bats, as you so charmingly describe them, are founder-members of this Club. Which means they've paid their subscriptions for over thirty years. So they're entitled to a little more consideration than a fourteen-year-old who hasn't paid a penny."

"Oh no, they're not!" They both turned in surprise, to see Lucy standing on the path a few feet away. Neither of them had noticed her approach. "There's nothing in the rules about founder-members having special privileges," she went on, "and juniors are supposed to have equal rights up to six o'clock."

The Major cleared his throat, obviously taken aback by this unexpected attack on his unguarded flank. "Yes, that's strictly true, Lucy," he said grudgingly. "But Mrs Bradley and her friends have done a great deal for this Club . . ."

"That's got nothing to do with it. If you expect *us* to stick to the rules, then so must you."

The Major began to retreat in the face of superior forces. "But this young feller's practising alone. He has no partner."

"He has now." Lucy marched to the gate and opened it.

"You're still only junior members . . ."

"*Only* junior members?" She rounded on him fiercely. "That's typical, that is. How d'you expect this country to produce world-beaters if people like you treat us like second-class citizens? It this was America, *we'd* be the ones with special privileges, not those four old . . . old bats."

She banged the gate behind her and stalked away towards the net. The Major shook his head, turned and vanished into the pavilion.

Barry couldn't understand why Lucy had come to his rescue. After their row the previous day, he would have thought she never wanted anything more to do with him. But he was grateful; her intervention had been decisive, and the old bats would now have to wait their turn.

He joined her at the net, where she was fixing a headband round her hair. "Proper little fire-cracker, in't you?" he said, grinning.

"I've been wanting to get that off my chest for a long time." She was still very angry. "They're prejudiced against juniors here—always hustling us off the courts. If they think we're such a drag, they shouldn't take our money."

"They don't take mine."

"Doesn't make any difference. If they accept you as a member, you have the same rights as everyone else."

"You want to play then?"

She smiled. "Haven't got much choice, have you? Frank asked me to tell you he's going to be late—so it's either me or no one."

Barry picked up a ball and bounced it on his racquet. "What I said yesterday. I was out of order. I didn't mean it."

"Neither did I. Come on—we'd better start using the court now I've made all that fuss."

They moved to opposite ends of the court and began to knock up. Barry concentrated on keeping the ball as low over the net as possible, and he found that Lucy, though she couldn't match his power, was every bit as accurate. The two men on the next court stopped to watch them, and Barry began to show off for their benefit, attempting impossible shots which, because he had nothing to lose, all came off. Lucy started to play with the same magical inspiration, and together they put on a demonstration that had the two spectators applauding enthusiastically.

It was while Barry was collecting the balls that he saw a familiar figure walking jauntily down the path towards him. He froze, rooted to the spot in astonishment. It was his father.

He waved, ran to the gate to greet him—but before he could open it, Major Houghton appeared, barring his way.

"Can I help you?"

Barry's heart sank. The Major's abrupt manner was bound to make his father's hackles rise. But his reply was mild enough. "My son," he said, jerking a thumb at Barry, "come to see him play."

"You're Mr Grieves?"

"Right. They tell me he's pretty good."

The Major stared at him coldly. "If only his manners were of the same standard."

Now there was bound to be bother, thought Barry. But luckily the Major turned on his heel and disappeared back into the pavilion.

His father sat down on a bench and nodded to Barry. "Now then. Let's see this great tennis player I've heard so much about."

Barry ran to the net, where Lucy was waiting patiently. "It's my Dad," he told her. "First time he's shown an interest."

"I'll send you some easy balls then. Make you look good."

He grinned. "Cheeky cow."

They moved back to the baselines and resumed their practice-session. But to Barry's dismay, he found that all his accuracy had gone. His drives, instead of zipping two or three inches over the net, now either caught the top of it or ballooned way out of court. And he could no longer get the angles right; if he aimed for the corners, the ball would fly out into the tramlines.

He started to play carefully, at half pace. But he found it more and more difficult to hit the ball cleanly. His shots felt cramped and awkward, his feet like lead. He tried hard to remember everything Frank had taught him—to give himself room, to keep a straight arm, to play the forehand off the left foot and the backhand off the right—but it was no use. For some mysterious reason, he had lost all his timing and technique.

He became hot and flustered, embarrassed by the appalling exhibition he was putting on in front of his father. Lucy, when they met at the net, told him to relax—but he couldn't. He knew what the old man was thinking—that if this was the best he could do, he was wasting his time. And it would be no use telling him this was an off-day, because he'd never believe it.

Barry was so busy trying to sort his game out that he didn't notice Frank walking down the path from the car park, accompanied by a short, thick-set man in a dark suit.

"Afternoon, Mr Grieves," said Frank, as they approached the bench on which Barry's father was sitting. "How's he doing?"

"Rotten. He's hardly got the ball over the net since I got here."

Frank frowned, turned to introduce his companion. "This is Mike Roper—a director of Benthall's. Barry's father."

Roper offered his hand. "Nice to meet you, Mr Grieves."

"Benthall's? The sports firm?"

"That's right. Frank suggested Barry as a suitable candidate for sponsorship. So I've come down to take a look at him."

Mr Grieves stared up at him. "You mean you might bung him some free gear?"

"If he's as good as Frank says he is."

"Pity we didn't know about you before. Barry's just laid out ninety quid."

Roper sat down next to him. "He'll soon grow out of those clothes. At his age, he'll need complete new outfits every year. Plus a regular supply of racquets and balls."

"And what do you get out of it?"

"Publicity."

"Worth your while, is it? I mean—it's not as if he was on the telly."

"It's early days yet. In a couple of years maybe . . ."

"No, this is just a hobby. He's going to give it up when he leaves school. Learn a trade."

Frank broke in quickly, trying to stop his carefully-laid plans from being sabotaged. "Well we're going to see how it goes, aren't we, Mr Grieves? Maybe Barry's trade'll turn out to be tennis."

Mr Grieves snorted derisively. "You're joking, Frank. I mean—look at him. He can't even beat this bird."

They watched in silence for a while. Barry continued to fluff his shots, making a series of unforced errors which Frank found inexplicable. He'd lost all his rhythm, all his confidence at the very moment when it mattered—*really* mattered.

Frank had purposely not told Barry that he was bringing Roper in case it might make him nervous. Despite this, the kid obviously *was* nervous—so either Lucy had told him Roper was coming, which Frank doubted because he'd expressly asked her not to . . . or it was nothing to do with Roper at all.

Out of the corner of his eye, Frank watched Mr Grieves shaking his head contemptuously as Barry drove an easy forehand into the net. He had to do something—and quickly.

"We're putting him off," he said, trying not to make the "we" sound like "you".

Mr Grieves glanced at him in disbelief. "Just by watching him? He's got to get used to spectators, hasn't he? If he's going to play in tournaments?"

Roper nodded. "That's true."

"Well I've got to be getting back." Mr Grieves stood up, patted Frank on the arm. "I hope you know what you're doing, Frank. But it looks like you're wasting your time." He walked off down the path.

Frank breathed a sigh of relief and sat down next to Roper who continued to watch Barry with a critical eye. "You're certainly wasting your time if the poor kid's got a parent-problem," he said thoughtfully. Frank, who had had to cope with many such problems, was forced to agree.

Roper leaned back on the bench and spread his arms out

along the back. "I don't fancy it. If there's family opposition, we don't like getting involved. And I can't say I'm impressed by what I've seen so far."

"He just got the elbow," Frank told him. "Stick around."

The change in Barry's game since the departure of his father was dramatic. His confidence came flooding back, and with it his natural rhythm and fluency. Hard, low drives began to flow from his racquet, falling just inside the baseline with unerring accuracy. It was hard to believe it was the same player who had been so clumsy and inept a few minutes before.

Roper nodded appreciatively, his interest suddenly rekindled. "Scared of his old man, eh?"

"Not scared," said Frank. "Trying to prove something. And pressing too hard."

"Same old story."

"All he needs is time."

But Roper sounded doubtful. "I dunno, Frank. If he's going to leave the game in a couple of years . . ."

"He's not. Not if I can help it."

"But you're not his father."

Frank sighed. "True."

"And he's an unknown quantity. I couldn't commit the Company till he's got a couple of tournaments under his belt."

Frank thought for a moment. He knew it was too soon, but Barry badly needed a sponsor; and if this was the only way he could get one, then so be it.

"All right," he said reluctantly. "I'll enter him for the County Under-sixteens." Ready or not, the kid would have to take his chances.

Barry, however, had no doubts. When Frank told him he was to compete in his first tournament, he reacted like a boxer who'd just been given a shot at the World Title, announcing his intention of wiping his opponents off the court.

He was sitting with Frank and Lucy in the pavilion after Roper had left. He and Lucy were halfway through their second cans of lemonade; Frank had almost finished his pint of beer. Major Houghton was leaning on the bar, puffing at his pipe and glowering at them through clouds of smoke.

Things were coming right after all, thought Barry. A chance to compete in the County Under-sixteens more than made up for his disappointment at having played so badly in front of his father. And as for Lucy—she wasn't at all the toffee-nosed fancy-knickers he had supposed. Like him, she was a fighter; and he had admired the way she'd told the Major where he got off. He wasn't yet sure what made her tick, but she was definitely someone to be reckoned with, both on and off the court.

Frank drained his glass and wiped the foam from his beard. "What about your father, Barry? You'll need his permission."

"No problem." Barry was by no means sure of this, but he wasn't going to share his doubts with Frank. "The tournament's in my half-term week, right? So I won't be missing school."

"Well, I'll leave it to you." Frank stood up, then frowned and looked embarrassed. "But there's something else . . ."

"What?"

"Ask him not to come."

Barry stared up at him. "Dad? Why?"

"This first tournament—it's important. And I think he might distract you."

"But I want him to come. I want him to see me win."

"There'll be plenty of time for that."

Barry thought for a moment. He desperately wanted to prove to his father that he really could play, but maybe Frank was right. Maybe he ought to concentrate on winning this tournament. "OK," he said, "I don't expect it'll break his heart."

"Let me know what he says. See you tomorrow." Frank picked up his bag and, with a nod to the Major, went out.

Lucy stared after him with a puzzled expression. "Funny," she said softly.

Barry glanced at her curiously. "What?"

"He never asked *me* to stop my parents coming."

"Yeh, well they talk proper, don't they? Maybe my old man hasn't got the right accent."

She shook her head. "Frank doesn't care how people talk."

"So what *does* he care about?"

"Winning."

Barry picked up his can of lemonade. "That makes two of us."

"Three of us."

There was a grim, determined look in Lucy's face that always seemed to appear when she was challenged—the "fire-cracker" expression Barry had seen when she was giving the Major a piece of her mind.

He grinned at her. "You? A half-pint no-no who can't hardly see over the net?"

She grinned back. "With the great Barry Grieves to practise with, how can I miss?"

"I'll drink to that," said Barry, raising his lemonade can.

Lucy raised hers. "To the winners!"

And they clinked their cans together, their differences forgotten and a friendship begun.

SIX

"Barry Grieves to Court Four please ... Barry Grieves to Court *Four immediately* ..."

Frank stood in front of the pavilion with Roper, looking round anxiously. This was the third time Barry had been called over the Tannoy, but there was still no sign of him. If he didn't answer this call, he'd be disqualified.

Where the hell was he? Frank had driven him to the North Ealing Club, where the County Under-sixteen Championships were being held, so he knew he was around somewhere. Surely he must have heard the announcement ...?

Roper was puzzled too. "That's the third call," he said, staring round the courts where the young competitors were battling for places in the Semi-Finals.

"I don't understand it," said Frank. "He was here a quarter of an hour ago."

"Changing room?"

"No. I've looked."

Roper was obviously becoming extremely irritated. "Well you'd better try and round him up, Frank. I don't fancy coming all the way out here for nothing."

*

Barry had forgotten all about the tournament. One of the other competitors had produced a football, and they had started a four-a-side game on the waste ground behind the pavilion. They had arranged that whichever side scored five goals would be the winner, and at the moment his team were leading by four goals to three.

He was dribbling past the opposition, about to make the winning score, when a voice he recognised made him stop dead in his tracks.

"Barry!"

He turned, saw Frank approaching from the direction of the pavilion with a face like thunder. "What the hell d'you think you're doing? They've been calling your match for ten minutes."

Barry blinked. He'd been so engrossed in the game, he'd lost all sense of time. "Oh—sorry. Which court?"

"Four. Get your skates on, or you'll be disqualified."

Frank was obviously very angry, so Barry hurried past him, collected his racquet which he'd left propped up against a tree and ran round the pavilion to Court Four.

His opponent—a boy called Chetwyn—was favourite to win the event. Barry had watched him play in one of the earlier rounds, and had not been particularly impressed. He was steady, and had no obvious weaknesses, but lacked power—so he rarely came to the net, preferring a defensive, baseline game.

Barry reckoned that anyone who could dominate the net could take him, and that was the plan he intended to adopt. But he had noticed something else about Chetwyn; whenever he was in trouble, he resorted to gamesmanship—delaying his next service in order to re-tie his shoelace, making audible remarks about his opponent's appearance, and so on. And he had called several balls out that were plainly in. So Barry was very much on his guard.

Chetwyn, tall and slim, was waiting impatiently for him on the court. "Oh, there you are," he drawled arrogantly as Barry arrived. "I was just about to claim a walk-over."

Trying to wind me up, thought Barry. "Sorry to disappoint you, sunshine," he said nonchalantly. "If you want a place in the Semis, you'll have to earn it."

Chetwyn studied him in silence for a moment, twirling his racquet. "You're new, aren't you?"

"New?"

"On the circuit. Your first tournament?"

"Yeh."

"And reached the Quarters, eh? Must've had an easy draw."

Barry was about to say that this looked like being the easiest match of the lot, but thought better of it. He'd come here to play tennis, not to take part in a debate.

He held out his racquet. "You want to call?"

"Smooth."

Barry spun his racquet, let it fall—then picked it up and inspected the strings. "It's rough," he announced.

"Let me see." Chetwyn grabbed the racquet and peered at it closely.

Barry stared at him in disbelief. "You don't trust me?"

"I don't know you, do I? Some of these kids—they'll cheat their own grandmothers."

"Satisfied?"

Chetwyn nodded. "Going to serve, are you?"

"Course."

"I'll take that end, then."

After a short knock-up, they began to play. Chetwyn returned Barry's first serve into the net. The second serve was a clean ace down the centre line, and Barry moved back to the right-hand court, ready for his next service.

But to his surprise, Chetwyn remained where he was. "Where d'you think you're going?" he called.

Barry wondered what on earth he was playing at. "It's thirty-love, right?"

"Fifteen-love. That serve was out."

"You're joking."

Chetwyn walked forward and pointed with his racquet. "There's the mark."

Barry put his hands on his hips and glared across the net. "You blind or something? That ball was a foot in."

"It's my call, old son. We don't have an umpire, so we have to mark our own cards."

Barry looked round, saw Frank standing with Roper by the side of the court and raised his eyebrows at him in a silent demand for support. But Frank said nothing; he remained quite still, his arms folded, staring expressionlessly back at him.

Realising he had no alternative but to replay the point, Barry walked reluctantly back to the left-hand court and served again. But he had lost his concentration; still thinking about the injustice he had suffered, he served the second ball tamely into the net. Chetwyn smiled. "Fifteen all," he called maliciously, and crossed to take up the opposite receiving position, twirling his racquet with deft, well-practised fingers.

Barry took a deep breath. I mustn't let him get to me, he thought. And, concentrating as hard as he could, he served three aces in a row which even Chetwyn hadn't the nerve to call out.

As they changed ends, however, his opponent produced another ploy from his bag of tricks. "Service action's not bad," he said, wiping his face lightly with a towel, "only you're throwing the ball too high."

This was easily countered. "They seemed to go in all right," replied Barry drily. "Including the one you called out."

"Think you know it all, do you?"

Barry poked him in the chest. "Listen, old son. I don't stick me nose into your game, and you don't stick your nose into mine. OK?"

Chetwyn shrugged indifferently. "Suit yourself."

As they walked away towards the baselines, Roper turned to Frank. "That second serve was well in."

"I know," said Frank, watching Barry intently.

"Why didn't you say something?"

"We're interested parties, so we can't interfere. Besides . . ."

"What?"

"I want to see how he handles it."

After several long, closely-fought rallies, Barry managed to reach game-point against Chetwyn's service. Chetwyn then decided that both his shoe-laces needed re-tying, and spent nearly a minute attending to them.

Barry waited with mounting impatience. He'd been expecting this, but even so it was intensely irritating. He paced backwards and forwards, trying to keep his concentration, but as the break in play lengthened, his temper rose.

"You want *me* to tie em for you?" he shouted angrily.

Chetwyn remained completely calm. "Can't help it," he called back, "it's these new laces."

"Funny they always seem to come loose at game-point against you, innit?"

"My. We *are* getting uptight, aren't we?" Chetwyn finally stood up and prepared to serve.

The return should have been a piece of cake. It was a gentle ball, on Barry's backhand, asking to be driven down the line into the open court. It was the sort of shot that Barry had made successfully hundreds of times in practice—but now he made a complete hash of it. His racquet sliced across the ball, sending it spinning out into the tramlines.

He flung the racquet to the ground in frustration. He was furious—both with Chetwyn for his blatant gamesmanship, and with himself for allowing it to upset him.

His next two returns caught the net—and a game which he had high hopes of winning was lost. One-all instead of two-love! In a towering rage, he picked up the balls and slammed them as hard as he could towards Chetwyn, who had to duck to avoid them. When Chetwyn straightened up and grinned at him, he knew he'd played straight into his opponent's hands. He told himself to relax and calm down. But his temperature had soared way above boiling point, and with a lousy cheat on the other side of the net, there seemed no way of bringing it down again.

Roper, who had watched Barry's childish display with growing disapproval, shook his head in disgust. "Stupid," he said quietly.

Frank glanced at him in alarm. Surely a man of his experience could make allowances? "It's his first tournament."

"He's got a couple of wins under his belt. He should've settled down by now."

Frank sighed. He was bitterly disappointed in Barry; they'd discussed Chetwyn and his dirty tricks, for which he was well-known on the junior circuit, so they should have come as no surprise. Yet Barry had fallen for them, revealing that under that brash exterior he was still desperately unsure of himself.

"I don't understand it," said Frank sadly. "He knew what to expect."

Roper watched Barry serve his second double-fault in a row. "But not how to cope."

"I hoped he'd work that out for himself."

"Asking rather a lot, weren't you? He's obviously still wet behind the ears. And Chetwyn's a shark—he's gobbled up bigger fish than your lad."

Frank silently cursed himself for not giving Barry firmer guidance. But it was a problem—a grey area in which he and his wife Judy took opposite points of view. How far could a tennis coach go without encroaching on parental territory? Judy, a teacher in a primary school, believed strongly that if Frank thought one of his pupils had a personality-defect, then it was his duty to try and cure it.

But Frank had always felt, equally strongly, that he should resist the temptation to interfere in his pupils' private lives. It simply wasn't his business. Though he had to admit that in the case of Alan Poskett, Judy had been right; if he *had* interfered, the lad might not be serving a six months' sentence in Borstal.

So maybe he should have done more to prepare Barry psychologically. Watching him now, flailing wildly at the ball and ruining his chances of Roper's sponsorship, Frank made up his mind not to make the same mistake again. He'd take the kid more firmly under his wing, even if it meant stepping on his father's toes.

The match was now a foregone conclusion. Barry had lost all control—over his racquet and his temper. He knew he was playing into Chetwyn's hands, but he couldn't help himself; there seemed to be a malignant devil inside him which had a will of its own.

Chetwyn served—an ace, swerving away to the forehand, out of Barry's reach.

"Fault," said the little devil.

Chetwyn grinned at him, unperturbed. "Sure about that, are you?"

"As sure as you was about that other call."

Chetwyn shrugged, served again with a lot of spin. The ball kicked wickedly, glancing off the end of Barry's racquet into the side-netting.

And so it went on—with Barry questioning Chetwyn's line

decisions, screaming at himself when he muffed a shot, and flinging his racquet all over the court. In contrast, Chetwyn now became a model of good behaviour, offering to play the point again if Barry contested one of his calls, and waiting patiently while Barry wandered round the court, muttering furiously to himself. He could afford to relax; it was all over bar the shouting.

As Barry missed another easy volley and hacked at the net in anger, Roper turned away. "I've seen enough, Frank," he said grimly. Then, as they started to walk towards the car-park: "He's got no self-control. We can't sponsor a kid who throws his racquet about like that. It'd be bad for our image."

He was absolutely right, thought Frank—but he felt bound to try and make him change his mind. "It's early days yet, Mike. He's still very green."

"So come back to me when he starts to mature."

"A sponsor could speed the process. Give him a sense of responsibility."

Roper shook his head. "We both know it doesn't often work like that. Some of these kids—they have it so easy, they become little prima donnas."

"Barry doesn't have it easy," said Frank quietly.

"Maybe not. But I'd like to see him sort out some of his problems before I commit myself. Let me know when you want me to take another look."

"Right."

They shook hands, and Roper climbed into his car and drove off. Frank walked slowly back to Court Four, deep in thought; Judy would approve of what he was about to do, but he wasn't looking forward to it. It would be very painful, and he might well find himself out of his depth.

He arrived back at the court just in time to see Chetwyn finish off the match with a crisp volley and offer his hand across the net. Barry, standing in mid-court, glowered at him. "Shove it," he said loudly.

The handful of spectators glanced at each other, shocked. Chetwyn played up to them, raising his eyebrows in mock surprise. "Bad loser, eh?"

"I don't fancy losing to cheats." This caused another shocked reaction from the spectators.

Chetwyn's tone changed. "You want to come over here and repeat that?" he asked silkily.

"Yeh." Barry could hardly wait to smash that grinning face to a pulp. He started to climb over the net.

But Frank had no intention of allowing this to develop into a free-for-all. "Barry!" he called sharply.

Barry suddenly seemed to remember where he was. Sheepishly, he turned and left the court. Frank met him at the gate. "Come on," he said grimly.

"Where're we going?"

"Back to my flat."

Barry felt a chill of apprehension. Judging by the expression on the coach's face, it looked as if he was going to be given his cards!

*

Lucy, meanwhile, was engaged in a titanic struggle on Court Ten, which had already lasted over an hour and a half.

She had never played Pam Summers before, though she had watched her many times, and admired her style. Pam was a tall, athletic girl with beautifully-produced groundstrokes who had a reputation as a brittle competitor. If she felt she had the measure of her opponent, she was unstoppable; but she would often collapse in the face of determined opposition.

So Lucy had decided that even if she was completely outplayed in the first set, she was going to hang in there as long as she could, in the hope that eventually cracks would begin to appear in Pam's game.

But the blitz had lasted longer than she expected. She had lost the first set six–one, and was five–six down in the second, so the situation was serious but not hopeless. If she could just take Pam's service, they'd be into a tie-break—and then anything could happen.

Lucy's mother was watching, sitting next to Pam's mother, so she was determined to do well. To reach the Quarter-Finals had been quite an achievement—and it would be no disgrace to lose to Pam, who was number five in the Under-sixteen rankings—but she had no intention of resting on her laurels. She was convinced she could win, if only she could get back into the match.

Red in the face, she scampered from side to side, running every ball down and getting it back into court, waiting for Pam to make a few mistakes. But she had had to wait a long time, and the situation had become very hairy. If she lost this game, it would be all over.

She was pleased that her mother had come; it made her feel she wasn't alone, that she was fighting not just for herself, but for the family. Some of the other girls, however, hated their parents watching them. Pam, for instance—before their match, she had confessed that when her mother was there she sometimes became a bundle of nerves.

Lucy couldn't understand this. What was the point of winning if the people you cared about didn't see you? So she always played better when her mother was there; the adrenalin ran faster, which gave her more energy. Though she did wish her mother's attention didn't wander so much; whenever she glanced at her, she always seemed to be looking at something else, whereas Mrs Summers never took her eyes off the game.

Pam sent a backhand drive screaming down the line. Lucy

watched it with dismay—she had no chance of reaching it—but it was just too long. She breathed a sigh of relief; thirty–forty! One more point and the game was hers.

She wiped her forehead on her wristlet, and crouched low to receive the next service. Pam's back arched gracefully; because of her height, which she used well, she was able to make her serves bounce head-high. So Lucy had two choices—either to stand well in and take the ball early, risking an error, or to stay back and wait for it, allowing her opponent to gain the advantage of the net position.

For this crucial serve, she decided to stay back. She watched the ball carefully, making sure her return went back into court—but as soon as she looked up, she realised it had been the wrong decision, Pam was already at the net, waiting confidently to make an easy kill.

Incredibly, she missed it—swiping the ball away into the tramlines. A gift from the gods, thought Lucy. Now it was six-all—and they were into the tie-break.

By the side of the court, the two mothers were reacting very differently. Mrs Roberts, unaware of the score, smiled encouragingly at Lucy. She was bored to tears with tennis, and only came because Lucy seemed to want her there. And because there'd be a tremendous row if she didn't. She always went to see Wendy act, so she supposed Lucy had a right to demand the same support.

Mrs Summers, however, seemed to be intensely interested. She behaved as if the future of the world depended on the outcome, vigorously applauding her daughter's good shots, and clicking her tongue in irritation at her mistakes.

While Pam was towelling down after losing her service, Mrs Summers called out to her angrily, "For heaven's sake, Pam. You threw that game away . . !"

"I know, Mother," said Pam coldly, "I don't need you to tell me."

"Well, just pull yourself together. You should never have let this set go to a tie-break!"

Pam's mouth tightened. She flung her towel down and stalked back to the baseline, ready to receive Lucy's service.

Mrs Roberts turned to Mrs Summers. "This tie-break thing—I never understand it. How does it work?"

Mrs Summers stared at her incredulously, amazed that a mother with a tennis-playing daughter could be so ignorant. "It's the first to reach seven points. Unless it's six-all—then it's whoever gets two ahead."

"I see." Mrs Roberts watched Pam return Lucy's serve into the net. "So that's one–nil to Lucy."

Mrs Summers bit her lip angrily. "I wish Pam had your girl's temperament."

"At least her skirt's a decent length! Lucy's is much too short, don't you think? I keep asking her to let me alter it."

Mrs Summers appeared not to have heard her. She hissed angrily as Pam served a double fault and called loudly: "Don't try for aces, you stupid girl! Just keep the ball in play, and let *her* make the mistakes."

Mrs Roberts couldn't imagine why she was getting so excited. She glanced round the other courts, where white-clad figures contorted themselves into unnatural shapes, stretching, twisting, leaping. "Nice club, isn't it?" she said wistfully. "Just like the old days."

"Old days?"

"When everyone wore whites. I hate these modern track-suits, don't you? So badly cut, most of them."

Mrs Summers ignored her, jumping to her feet and shouting as Pam muffed an easy forehand. "What sort of a shot is that? Head up, bent arm, completely off-balance. You're supposed to be playing tennis, Pam, not swatting flies."

"My husband proposed to me at a tennis club, you know." Mrs Roberts was still lost in a world of her own. "He looked so elegant, I just couldn't turn him down." Then, sharply. "But if he'd popped the question in a tatty track-suit, he'd 've got a very different answer, I can tell you."

She was talking to herself. Mrs Summers, tense with fury, was shouting at her daughter again. "Rubbish! Don't watch your opponent, watch the ball!"

Mrs Roberts thought it was about time she showed some interest. "What's the score now?" she asked pleasantly.

"It's set point against Pam."

They watched as Lucy produced a backhand passing shot that left Pam stranded. Mrs Summers was furious. "What's the matter with you?" she hissed, as Pam approached for the changeover at the end of the set. "You're playing like a beginner."

"Oh, shut up, Mother!" Without pausing to towel herself down, Pam marched away again.

With the second set in the bag, Lucy began to play with renewed confidence. At the same time, Pam's game started to disintegrate; and she seemed to lose interest, providing only token opposition. The tide had turned, and Lucy raced through the set, winning it six–love.

As they shook hands at the end of the match, Pam was blinking back tears. Lucy felt sorry for her; she knew what it was like when you couldn't seem to do anything right, when all the luck seemed to run against you. Tennis players at all levels suffered similar bad patches occasionally; there was nothing you could do about it except wait for the gods to decide you'd taken enough punishment.

But Pam's bad patch, she was sure, had not been caused by the gods. No one could play under the sort of pressure her mother was putting on her. At least Lucy could never accuse *her* mother of getting uptight.

Her sympathy for Pam, however, was soon forgotten in the joy of victory. And the fact that her mother had seen it made her triumph all the sweeter. Lucy hoped she realised how important it was; to beat the number five-ranked girl in the Under-sixteen Division was a real achievement. It meant that she was now well and truly on the national tennis map, and that she would probably qualify for Regional Squad training later in the year—an honour that all the girls prized.

As they came off the court, Pam avoided her mother's eye. "Sorry," she mumbled miserably.

"Sorry?" Mrs Summers stared at her contemptuously. "What's the use of being sorry?"

"I don't know what went wrong. I just couldn't get it together."

"I'll tell you what went wrong—the same thing that always goes wrong! As soon as someone fights back at you, you go to pieces. You've no backbone, that's your trouble."

Pam buried her head in her towel to hide her tears. Lucy and her mother waited, embarrassed and helpless.

Mrs Summers grabbed Pam by the arm. "Come on. I don't know what your father's going to say, I'm sure. We're beginning to run out of excuses." They walked off down the path.

Mrs Roberts kissed Lucy on the cheek. "Well done, darling. That was the Semi-Final, was it?"

"Quarter-Final."

"Oh."

"Something the matter?"

"That means it's the Semi-Final tomorrow, and the Final on Saturday?"

"That's right."

"I promised Wendy I'd take her down to Brighton on Saturday afternoon. Some boy she's rather keen on is in a play there."

Lucy was deeply hurt. Surely her sister's love-life could take second place for once? "Just have to hope I don't get to the Final then, won't we?" she said bitterly.

"Don't be silly, dear. I'm very proud of you. But there's just one thing . . ."

"What?"

"Your skirt. It really is too short, you know. You don't realise how embarrassing it is for me."

Lucy could hardly believe her ears.

SEVEN

"Sit down."

Barry sat. Frank hadn't spoken during the drive back to his flat, so it was difficult to estimate how angry he was. But his first words left no doubt: "If you ever—repeat *ever*—behave like that again, you can find yourself another coach. Clear?"

"It was that Chetwyn," said Barry sullenly. "He's a con-merchant."

"He's not the only one on the circuit. So you'd better get used to 'em."

"You mean I've just got to swallow it?"

Frank contemplated him in silence for a moment, then turned and began to pace round the room. It was a small, airy flat in a modern apartment block near the park. In a corner stood a workbench, with a vice holding a half-strung racquet. On the walls hung several pictures of Frank holding cups and trophies that he'd won—a young, athletic Frank smiling at the camera with flashing teeth, eyes screwed up against the suns of past summers. Some of the trophies decorated the mantelpiece, surrounding a wedding photograph of Frank and his wife—a small, slim, dark woman—gazing into each others' faces outside a church.

Barry would have liked to have inspected the cups and photos more closely, but there was no time for that now.

Frank was obviously determined to give him an ear-bashing, and he had to pay attention.

"Listen, Barry. You want to be a winner, don't you?"

"Course!"

"Then you've got to learn to keep your cool! The moment you let your opponent needle you, you become a loser."

Barry shrugged. "They don't keep their cool at Wimbledon. I've seen 'em—effing and blinding at the linesmen, the umpire, the crowd . . ."

"Ever seen Borg do that?"

Barry had to admit he hadn't. The Swedish iceberg never seemed to show a flicker of emotion.

Frank sat opposite him. "And have you ever seen any of his opponents try to con him out of a match?"

"No."

"Because they know it wouldn't work, that's why. They'd just be making fools of themselves."

"But I'm not like Borg," Barry protested. "If I can't let it all hang out, I'd blow me top."

"You don't have to be a saint. But if you show your opponent he's getting to you, you're giving him a tremendous psychological advantage. So rule number one of match play is never let the other bloke know what you're thinking. Or how you're feeling."

Barry glanced round at the photos on the walls. "That's how *you* used to play it, eh? When you was on the circuit?"

Frank followed his gaze, staring critically at the images of his youth as if they were strangers. "Not at first. I used to carry on just like you did today . . ."

Barry was suddenly interested; the possibility that Frank had once been an effer and blinder had never occurred to him. "So what changed *you* into a bleeding iceberg?"

"I was never that. But one day my Dad gave me a piece of advice. The same advice I'm going to give to you . . ."

"A right rollicking?"

Frank smiled. "That's only part of it."

"Come on, then. Get it over with."

The smile faded, to be replaced by a long, cool stare. "Why d'you think people take up sport, Barry?"

"Lots of reasons. To get fit, earn money, find out how good they are . . ."

"You've left out the main one."

"What's that?"

"Enjoyment."

"So."

"Did you enjoy yourself today?"

The memory of his disgrace returned, and Barry gritted his teeth. "Would *you* enjoy losing to a creep like Chetwyn?" Then, surprising himself by the intensity of his feeling, "Winning—that's the only thing that turns me on."

Frank surveyed him thoughtfully for a moment, then shook his head. "There are more important things."

"Such as?"

"You. Your development as a person."

"That's a bit heavy, innit? From a tennis coach?"

"I'd hoped I was more than that."

"Not if you start with all them verbals. That's what I get from me old man."

"I'm just trying to give you a sense of proportion, Barry. Competitiveness is all very well, but it has to be channelled and controlled. Otherwise, you'll have a miserable life."

"Eh?" Barry wondered what on earth Frank was on about. OK, so he'd blown the match. The last thing he needed was a sermon.

But a sermon was apparently what he was going to get. "The game's bigger than any one player," Frank went on, "no matter how good he is. So you have to play it for its own sake—you can't just use it as a way of getting out from under."

"Why not?"

"Because you'll never be free. You'll always be a prisoner of your own fears. And you'll never be a winner."

This is getting heavier and heavier, thought Barry. "What's wrong with making money out of something you're good at?" he demanded, beginning to resent being treated like a kid at Sunday school.

"Nothing's wrong with it—as long as making money isn't your first objective. If it is, then con-merchants like Chetwyn will always be able to make a mug out of you."

The hairs on the back of Barry's neck began to bristle. "So I'm a mug, eh?"

"You're a young mug. I'm trying to stop you growing into an old one."

Barry had heard enough; he wasn't going to take any more of this rubbish. "Right," he said grimly, jumping to his feet, "that's it, then."

Frank looked taken aback. "What?"

"I don't need a coach who thinks I'm a mug. A feller who reckons there's something dirty about wanting to get rich."

"Oh, come on, Barry. I didn't say that . . ."

"Me old man was right. Tennis *is* a snobby game. And you're just as snobby as the rest." He knew this was untrue, but he was past caring.

Frank stood up, still trying to get through to him. "I wasn't talking about tennis—I was talking about all sport. If footballers don't enjoy their football, they might as well go down the pits."

"Some of 'em take up football to get *out* of the pits. But you wouldn't know about that, would you?"

"Wouldn't I?"

"No. If you had your way, there'd be no professional sport at all. There'd only be bleeding amateurs, larking about for free."

"That's childish," said Frank wearily. "You obviously haven't been listening . . ."

Barry pushed past him and opened the door—then turned back, shaking with fury. "You said I was using tennis to get out from under," he heard himself saying. "Well, you was right. And if that gets up your nose, you can take a running jump. I'll make it on me own."

He went out, slamming the door behind him. But outside the flat he paused, the devil inside him now purged. What on earth had made him lose his rag like that? Once again, he'd made a fool of himself—and this time he'd done some real damage, because he'd blown the best chance he had of avoiding the dole queues.

He knew it was an empty boast—he'd never make it on his own. Yet now he *was* alone—completely alone—and it was his own fault. In the depths of despair, he started to walk slowly down the stairs.

*

When Lucy arrived home, the last person she wanted to see was Wendy. But her sister was sprawled on the living-room sofa, reading *The Stage*.

She looked up as Lucy and her mother entered. "Well, Beetle? Did you win?"

Lucy, in a black mood, flung herself into a chair. "What do you care?"

Her mother, helping herself to a sherry, looked shocked. "Lucy! Don't be such a grouch. A civil question deserves a civil answer."

"It's all right, Mother," said Wendy maliciously, "I *quite* understand."

Lucy glowered at her. "Understand what?"

"Why you don't want to talk about it."

"Oh? And why's that?"

"Well, you obviously lost. Otherwise you wouldn't be so grumpy."

"Wrong, Clever-Clogs."

Wendy's beautiful eyes widened. "You won? Then why on earth didn't you say so?"

" 'Cos you're not really interested," said Lucy sulkily.

"Who says I'm not?"

"You make it so obvious."

Mrs Roberts carried her glass of sherry to a chair, and sat down with a sigh of weariness. "Darling, you're being very unreasonable. If Wendy wasn't interested, she wouldn't have bothered to ask, would she?"

"She'd have made some snide remark. She always does."

"Like what?" demanded Wendy from the depths of the sofa.

"Like the one you made when I got through the first round. That the other girl must've had a wooden leg."

"That was meant to be a joke. You know—funny ha-ha."

"Well I didn't think it was funny."

"You've got no sense of humour." Wendy threw down *The Stage* and sat up. "Honestly, Beetle, I don't know what's the matter with you lately. If you're like this when you win, God help us when you lose."

Lucy could think of nothing to say to this, so she stuck her tongue out at her sister. A childish reaction, of which she was immediately ashamed.

Her mother frowned at her. "I think you're letting this tennis business get on top of you, Lucy. Maybe you should forget about it for a while. Take up something else."

"I'm not good at anything else."

"How d'you know till you try? In any case, there's no harm in broadening one's horizons. You may find some other hobby you like better."

Lucy jumped to her feet, her eyes blazing. "Hobby? Tennis isn't my *hobby*, mother."

"What is it, then?"

"It's my . . ." she tried to think of the right word . . . "my *life*."

"Oh come! Don't you think that's a little melodramatic?"

Wendy laughed. "You wait a couple of years, Beetle—wait till you start getting interested in boys. You'll find they're much more fun than tennis."

Lucy rounded on her furiously. "Oh don't be so pompous." And she stormed out of the room.

*

It was just after eight o'clock when Frank heard Judy's key in the lock. For an hour and a half, ever since Barry left, he had sat by the window, watching the shadows lengthen across the allotments, where shirt-sleeved elderly men were digging, forking and watering.

He needed to talk to Judy. At first he had wondered why she was so late; then he remembered she was at a meeting of the Parent-Teachers Association. So he just sat waiting for her in the gathering darkness, too depressed to heat up the supper which he knew she would have left in the oven.

He'd lost Alan Poskett through failing to follow Judy's advice; was he now going to lose Barry by taking it? It seemed so unfair—whatever he did turned out to be wrong, to end in some kind of disaster. And yet in Barry's case, surely he'd been right to read him the Riot Act? So many kids failed to make it because they lacked temperament and self-control, even when they possessed every shot in the book. Better to lose him than allow him to destroy himself.

No, Frank couldn't think of any reason why he need reproach himself. Yet reproach himself he did—which was why he needed Judy's seal of approval. She never seemed to be tortured by doubt; once she'd made up her mind, she was firm and undeviating.

She switched on the light, and gave a little start as she saw him. Then she frowned, knowing instinctively that something was wrong. "Frank? What are you doing?"

"Thinking," he told her.

"What about?"

"Barry Grieves."

She walked slowly over to him. "Something happened?"

"I blew the whistle on him today. And he walked out on me."

"What did you say?"

"That there were more important things than winning."

Without taking her eyes off him, she threw down the pile of exercise books she was carrying. "*You* said *that*?"

Frank gave her a wry smile. "Yes. I'm surprised it didn't stick in my throat."

"What made you see the light?"

"I've always seen it. But it's not my job to point it out to my pupils. For some of them, it could be positively dangerous."

"Why?"

"I'm a tennis coach, for God's sake. I should be telling them there's *nothing* more important than winning."

"But in this case, you didn't?"

"No. For the first time I took your advice and stepped into a parent's shoes. I wish I'd kept my big mouth shut."

Judy sank into a chair and put her legs up on the coffee table. "If you care about someone and you think they're going off the rails, you can't just stand back and do nothing. You have to speak out."

She was providing the reassurance Frank was hoping for, but he continued to play devil's advocate. "I don't have the right, Judy. The kid doesn't belong to me."

"You've devoted a lot of time to him. That gives you some right."

"Suppose I destroyed his will to win? Turned him into a well-behaved loser? It would be unforgivable."

"It would be even more unforgivable to ignore his faults."

He glanced at her sharply. "We're back to Alan Poskett, are we?"

"Alan Poskett would never have amounted to anything as a player, because no one took the trouble to straighten him out as a person. You tried to separate the two, and it was a disastrous mistake. This time you've done the right thing."

"With the wrong result."

"For you, perhaps. But not for him."

As usual, Judy was strong and positive. And despite his disappointment at losing his prize pupil, Frank knew she was right. So now there was no alternative but to wait. Give Barry time to absorb his lesson, and hope that it wouldn't be long before the lost sheep returned to the fold.

*

But summer turned to autumn, and Barry made no attempt to heal the rift between them. He had realised almost immediately that Frank was right, that he'd been a berk to walk out on him—but he had his pride. He wasn't going to go crawling back with his tail between his legs; having told his parents that he'd given Frank the elbow, it would be too humiliating. And his father, who had been delighted at the news, would rub his nose in it.

For the first couple of weeks after their row, Barry had hoped that Frank would call round, apologise for tearing him off a strip, and offer to resume the lessons. But he knew it was a forlorn hope, that he was the one who ought to make the first move—and he wasn't surprised when the call never came.

All through the summer holidays, he continued to practise with Lucy—but he knew he wasn't getting any better, that there were gaps in his knowledge of the game which he desperately needed to fill. Even so, he took care never to be at the Club when Frank was due to give a lesson there.

Lucy, whom he had grown to like and trust, told him not to be so stupid—that he was cutting off his nose to spite his face. She also acted as an intermediary between him and Frank, who, according to her, was quite willing to take Barry back if he asked him. But as time went on, it became more and more difficult to ask; with every day that passed, the breach seemed wider.

The autumn term began with another row. He refused to turn out for the Under-sixteen Football team, which provoked a confrontation, first with Mr Miller, then with the Headmaster. When he persisted in his refusal, the Headmaster had written to his father, asking him to persuade Barry to change his mind. But surprisingly, his father had taken Barry's side; calling the letter "a bleedin' liberty", he had replied that if his son didn't want to turn out for the school, then he wasn't going to interfere. There was no rule that said Barry *had* to play.

So the atmosphere in the classroom was hardly friendly. But at least they left him alone. "Muscles" virtually ignored him, and the members of the football team made no more attempts to put pressure on him.

One morning, three weeks after the beginning of term, he found Lucy waiting for him outside Mr Ferris's shop at the end of his paper round.

"Hi," she said, smiling.

"Hi." She looked so neat in her school uniform, he hardly recognised her. "You're up early."

"I know. I wanted to talk to you."

"What about?"

"Regional Squad training."

He frowned, puzzled. "Eh?"

"I've been selected." She took an envelope from her pocket and waved it under his nose. "Got a letter this morning from the L.T.A. Means the powers-that-be are starting to notice me."

"Congratulations," he said bitterly, and walked past her into the shop.

She followed him inside and tugged at this arm. "Hold on, Barry. I didn't come to gloat. I'm telling you because you ought to try and get on it too. It's a chance to meet all the right people."

Barry was intrigued. He was conscious that Mr Ferris was listening, but he didn't care. This was something he had to find out about. "What's it cost?" he asked.

"Nothing. You spend a week down at Bisham Abbey—that's near Marlow—all expenses paid."

"A week off school?" That would surely put the mockers on it. "The Headmaster wouldn't wear that. Neither would me old man."

"It's worth a try, isn't it?" Lucy's face was shining with excitement. "If you can get your name on the Regional Squad list, it'd show 'em both you're really getting somewhere."

Barry thought for a moment. If this Regional Squad training was as important as Lucy made it sound, then it certainly *was* worth a try. "So what do I have to do?"

"You have to be recommended by your coach."

He might have known there was a catch. "Forget it," he said grimly.

But Lucy wouldn't give up. "Yes, you're going to have to make it up with Frank," she told him solemnly. "If you don't, you're going to miss out. So if I were you, I'd eat a bit of humble pie . . ."

Throughout the rest of the day, Barry wrestled with the problem. It was crunch time—and he knew that if he didn't make a move now, he never would. He could picture himself as a middle-aged man bored out of his mind with some dull office or factory job, looking back on this moment and wondering how different his life might have been if he hadn't been so stubborn.

Lucy asked no questions during their practice-session that afternoon, and he was grateful for her tact. But he had already made his decision; he was going to go and see Frank that evening. He fully expected the coach would tell him to get lost, but it was a risk he had to take.

He walked straight to Frank's flat from the Club. His heart was racing wildly as he pressed the bell, part of him hoping there'd be no reply. Then the door was flung open, and there was Frank, staring at him expressionlessly.

Barry opened his mouth, but could think of nothing to say—so he shut it again. The silence seemed to go on for ever before Frank broke the ice. "Hello, Barry," he said quietly, "come in."

He stood aside to allow Barry to enter; then shut the door, and nodded towards a tray on the low table. "Cup of tea? It's still hot."

Barry didn't dare look at him. "Yeh. Ta."

Frank fetched a cup from the kitchen, and told him to sit down. "Well?" he asked, as he poured the tea. "What can I do for you?"

Barry swallowed nervously; it had been so many weeks since they'd met, they were almost like strangers. "That time when I lost me rag and walked out on you," he said, the words tumbling out in a rush, "I was out of order. Behaved like a right berk."

"True. But it was partly my fault. I shouldn't have hit you when you were down."

So far, so good, thought Barry; the door still seemed to be open. "Talked a lot of sense, though. I see that now."

Frank handed him the cup, then picked up his own and sipped it, taking his time. "I'll tell you why I did it, Barry. Couple of years ago, I took on another kid—someone very like you—with the same potential. And the same 'win at all costs' mentality."

"What happened?"

"He was a young villain. Nothing serious—but he had a police record for shoplifting. And when he was caught nicking money from the changing rooms at the Club, they prosecuted—and he was sent to Borstal."

Barry, who hadn't nicked anything from anybody for five years, wondered what this had to do with him. "So?" he asked.

"My wife blamed me," said Frank, staring at his cup. "She said I was partly responsible."

"Why?"

"Because I introduced him to an environment where temptation was put in his way. And I didn't make sure he resisted it."

"That wasn't down to you. What about his old man?"

"His old man was a villain too. So he got no guidance at home—and I didn't think I had the right to interfere. The poor kid had no chance."

Barry frowned. "And you reckon I could go the same way?"

"I'm not saying you're a potential villain, Barry. But you could ruin your career in other ways."

"And that's why you gave me that rollicking?"

Frank put down his cup and leaned back. "I was determined not to make the same mistake with you. I've learned my lesson; it's impossible *not* to concern myself with my pupils' private lives, because problems off the court often lead to problems on it."

"Yeh." Barry could see the logic of this; he never played well when he felt uptight about Mr Miller or his father.

For a long moment, neither of them spoke. But there was nothing awkward about the silence; their old relationship had been re-established, and they were once more at ease with each other.

Then Frank smiled. "I'm glad you came back. Even though I can guess the reason."

Barry blinked at him, startled. "Eh?"

"It couldn't have anything to do with the Regional Squad training, could it?"

"How d'you know?"

"The L.T.A. sent out their invitations yesterday. I wondered how long it'd be before you got to hear about them."

This took the wind out of Barry's sails. He had meant to introduce the subject casually, as if it wasn't important. But Frank was obviously not deceived, and the big question could not be delayed any longer.

"So? How about getting me on the list?"

"You're already on it."

Barry stared, open-mouthed. "How come I didn't get an invitation, then?"

"Because when I submitted your name, I didn't give them your address. So they sent the invitation to me." Frank produced a letter from his pocket, and held it up.

Barry's heart missed a beat as he saw the heading, printed in blue: THE LAWN TENNIS ASSOCIATION. BARON'S COURT. WEST KENSINGTON.

His excitement, however, was soured by indignation. "You mean—if I hadn't come crawling back, you'd never've let me know?"

Frank folded the letter and put it back in his pocket. "That's right."

"You bastard."

"I only recommend a pupil for Squad training if I think he or she is ready. As I couldn't seem to get through to you, I didn't think you *were* ready. So if you hadn't come back, I was going to withdraw your name."

Barry grinned. "Lucky I did then, wasn't it?"

"Lucky for both of us. I must admit, I was getting worried."

"There's just one problem . . ." Barry's grin faded, as he remembered the large obstacle that stood in the way of his dream.

"What?"

"Me old man . . ."

Frank offered to drive Barry home and talk to his father—who, to Barry's surprise, listened attentively while Frank explained the value of Squad training, and what an honour it was to be selected for it. On hearing that it meant taking a week off school, however, he shook his head.

"It's not on, Frank. He'll get behind with his work."

"I'll make it up, Dad," said Barry. "I promise."

"But I can't ask the Headmaster to give you that amount of time off. He's already written to me about this tennis lark."

"Bleedin' liberty! You said so yourself."

"Maybe. But from what I hear, you've made yourself pretty unpopular at school, Barry. And if you was to take a week's leave just to play tennis, they'd really have it in for you."

Frank looked contemptuous. "They obviously don't realise what it means to be selected for Regional Squad training. The school should be proud of him, not try to make him conform."

Mr Grieves thought for a moment. "So what goes on at this place, then?"

"Bisham Abbey? Barry'll get some intensive coaching, and he'll be assessed at national level. It's the break we've been waiting for."

"Break from his work and all. The headmaster'd go spare."

"And if he don't let me off, *I'll* go spare," said Barry desperately. "Talk to him, Dad—please."

His father stared at him. "Willing to take the fall-out, are you?"

"Yeh."

There was a long, agonising pause before the answer came. "OK. I'll give him a bell."

Barry sighed with relief. If his father was prepared to call the Headmaster, he reckoned he was on his way.

EIGHT

The bus set Barry and Lucy down opposite a driveway, and growled off down the Marlow Road like an angry bear. They carried their suitcases across to the notice just inside the wall.

"Funny," said Barry, staring at the smart blue board, "it don't say nothing about an abbey. Just Sports Council Training Centre. What else goes on here?"

"You name it. Football, table-tennis, squash—even dancing."

"Dancing? That's not a sport."

"You have to be fit, though. Fitter than most athletes."

They started to walk up the drive. It was a misty October afternoon, with a few gold and brown leaves still clinging to the trees as if fearful of the coming winter. Barry breathed deeply; it felt good to be in the country, even though the mist that shrouded the valley prevented him from seeing very far. It was so quiet after London; now they were away from the road, the only sounds were the bleating of sheep and their footsteps on the gravel.

And the week stretched invitingly. Just doing what he loved best, with no Mr Miller to hassle him—all for free! He realised how lucky he was, that other kids would sell their own grandmothers to get on a course like this. And to think he'd nearly missed it! If it hadn't been for Lucy, the whole thing would have passed him by. Yes, he thought gratefully, he definitely owed her one.

They passed some multi-coloured all-weather courts, where two tough-looking men were hitting the ball so hard it was invisible, and rounded the corner of a grey stone building to find themselves standing in a half-enclosed courtyard. Some distance away, on their left, was a complex of more modern structures, where Barry assumed all the various indoor activities took place.

There was a notice outside the main door of the Abbey saying UNDER-SIXTEEN TRAINING GROUP REGISTER HERE, so Barry and Lucy walked up to the entrance and through the imposing portico.

Just inside the door, a grey-haired female receptionist sat at a desk with a typewritten list in front of her. Beyond the desk was a wood-panelled dining-room, with long trestle tables laid for dinner. Barry had never seen anything like it except on television; it reminded him of the castle from which Robin Hood had rescued Maid Marion in some old movie they'd shown the previous year.

The receptionist's voice brought him abruptly back to the present. "Names please?"

"Lucy Roberts."

"Barry Grieves."

The receptionist ticked off their names on her list, and stood up. "Right. If you come with me, I'll show you to your rooms."

Barry couldn't resist trying to shock her. "Rooms?" he said in mock surprise. "You mean we're not sharing?"

The receptionist gave him a withering glance and moved to the door. Lucy's elbow dug into Barry's ribs. "Shut up, you fool," she whispered hoarsely, "she'll think you're a yobbo."

"I *am* a yobbo."

"In London, maybe. Here, you're one of the chosen few."

They followed the receptionist across the grass to a row of brick buildings which she called the dormitory block. Barry waited outside while she escorted Lucy to her room, then accompanied her to one of the dormitory-houses at the other end of the row.

He hadn't expected to have a room of his own, and was delighted when he saw it. Small, but clean and comfortable, with a view of trees and grass. Like a hotel, he thought, as he threw his suitcase on the bed and started to unpack; too good to be true.

Unfortunately, the gods agreed with him and decided to bring him down to earth with an unpleasant bump. He was stuffing his tennis gear into a drawer when a voice he recognised shattered his complacency.

"Well, well! If it isn't the bad loser . . ."

Barry whirled round, to see Chetwyn lounging nonchalantly in the doorway. "What do *you* want?" he asked coldly.

"Saw your name on the list, old son. So I thought I'd drop in and say hello."

"OK—you said it. Now shove off."

"That's not very nice . . ." Chetwyn wandered over to the bed and lay down on it, hands clasped behind his head. "We're going to be living next door to each other for a week, so we might as well try to get on."

"We'll get on all right—if you keep out of my way."

Chetwyn smiled mockingly. "Big Chief Grieves not prepared to smoke peace-pipe? What a shame." He picked up Barry's pyjamas and inspected them critically. "What an appalling taste in nightwear."

Barry snatched them away. "You conned me out of our match, Chetwyn," he said, his anger and resentment flooding back, "I'll never forget that."

"Like I said. A bad loser."

"If we'd had an umpire, you wouldn't have had a prayer."

Chetwyn swung himself up into a sitting position. "Cocky little sod, aren't you? And that's the thanks I get for going easy on you." He stood up and moved to the door. "Well next time we meet, you'd better watch out. 'Cos I'm going to give you a real spanking . . ."

It was a disappointing beginning to the week, but Barry was determined not to let Chetwyn's presence distract him. He'd waited so long for the chance to impress the National coaches, and he couldn't afford to blow it. If Chetwyn continued to needle him, however, it wasn't going to be easy.

All through dinner that evening, he concentrated on talking to Lucy. But every time he looked away from her, he seemed to catch Chetwyn's eye. It was a brooding, menacing presence which was impossible to ignore.

After dinner, the group of eight boys and eight girls gathered in the recreation room to be introduced to the two coaches who were to be in charge of their training programme; a man and a woman, both with impressive-looking L.T.A. badges on their track-suits.

"Welcome to Bisham Abbey," said the man. Dark and wiry, he stood with his feet apart and his hands clasped behind his back. "For those of you who don't know us, I'm Peter Hastings, and this . . ." indicating the blonde, athletic woman at his side . . . "is Sally Brewster. We're not just tennis coaches—we're here to help you—so if you have any problems, come to us, OK?"

He paused, looking round the ring of silent, attentive faces. Then his tone changed. "But if you think you're on to a cushy number here, you're in for a nasty shock. This isn't a holiday camp—you'll be working your socks off for six hours a day. So if any of you have been neglecting your stamina training lately, you're going to wish you hadn't . . ."

Barry, catching Lucy's eye, pulled a rueful face. Since his row with Frank, he'd started to take his paper round at a slow jog, and he realised he wasn't in such good condition as he had been at the beginning of the summer. He hoped he'd be able to last the pace.

"One other thing," Hastings continued, "don't start believing you're little tin gods and goddesses just because you've been selected for this course. In terms of tennis, you're standing on the bottom rung of the ladder—the lowest of the low—and even that may be too high for some of you. So there's nothing to get big-headed about. Any questions?"

There weren't any. The group seemed to have taken his words to heart, obviously believing that the lowest of the low should be seen but not heard.

"Right," said Hastings briskly, "we start tomorrow at nine o' clock. In the Workshop."

The Workshop turned out to be a large building containing four green-carpeted tennis courts. Next morning, the eight girls were assigned to two of the courts, knocking up under the watchful eye of Sally Brewster, while the eight boys were led through a series of punishing exercises by a bald Physical Training instructor built like a tank.

Barry endured the torture in silence, though his muscles shrieked in protest. But the others were more vocal in their suffering; there were groans of agony as they followed the instructor round the court, pausing only for knee-bends, star jumps or press-ups. "It's only the first day," gasped a boy called Francis, whom Barry had met at the North Ealing Club, "and I'm knackered already."

After what seemed an eternity, the instructor told them they could relax, and they collapsed in exhausted heaps on the green carpet. Barry glanced over at the girls, who were doing what *he* expected to be doing—playing tennis. What happened to equality he wondered, scowling at them? When the going got rough, they were quite happy to be treated differently. Lucy turned and grinned at him. Just you wait, he thought sourly; maybe your turn will come.

Hastings appeared on the court, twirling his racquet and looking down at the outstretched bodies without sympathy. "Cheer up," he said grimly, "only five hours forty minutes to go ..."

This was greeted by a chorus of groans, but the short rest-period was apparently over. "OK—on your feet," ordered Hastings. "And go and fetch your racquets ..."

This is more like it, thought Barry, as he ran to the spectators' stand by the side of the court and collected his racquet from one of the benches; now I'll show'em.

When they returned to the court, Hastings split them into groups of four for the rest of the morning session. Barry was told to partner Francis against Chetwyn and a red-haired boy called Riley. Before starting to play, however, they were to have half an hour's volleying practice—with all four boys standing inside the service line.

All went well while Hastings was watching, and Barry was able to demonstrate the speed of his reactions as the ball flew across the net in a four-cornered rat-tat-tat of volleys. But as soon as Hastings turned his attention to the adjoining court, Chetwyn seemed to forget about Francis and to aim all his shots straight at Barry. As long as the ball stayed low over the net, Barry had no difficulty in returning them; but when Francis, on one of the rare occasions he was allowed to join in a rally, sent a gentle lob looping over Chetwyn's head, there was no escape. Chetwyn could have sent the ball anywhere, but he smashed it straight at Barry with all his strength. It caught Barry in the stomach, doubling him up and sending him crashing down on to the court.

Hastings turned and hurried over to him, putting a solicitous hand on his shoulder. "OK, Barry?"

Barry, still winded, climbed slowly and painfully to his feet. "Just about."

Hastings handed him his racquet, gave him an encouraging pat on the back and moved away to the next court. Barry resumed his position inside the service line, glaring across the net at Chetwyn.

Chetwyn grinned at him. "Dangerous game, tennis."

"Yeh," said Barry darkly. He had no intention of letting him get away with it. Sooner or later, he would have his revenge.

The opportunity came sooner rather than later . . . during the next rally. This time it was Riley who mis-hit the ball, lobbing it up for Barry to make an easy kill. He didn't hesitate; angling his racquet, he smashed it straight at Chetwyn.

His aim was perfect. Chetwyn turned sideways to protect his stomach, but the ball caught him in the side and he gasped with pain, dropping his racquet and rubbing his bruised ribs.

"Sorry, old son," said Barry cheerfully, "dangerous game, tennis."

But his triumph was short-lived. He turned, to find Hastings beckoning to him, his face like thunder. "Come here, Barry . . ."

Barry walked slowly over to him with a sinking heart. He had thought Hastings was still watching the other court, but he seemed to have witnessed the whole incident. Which was both bad luck and bad news.

"If you ever do that again," said Hastings softly, "you're on the next bus home. Understand?"

"He did it to me," said Barry, staring down at his feet.

"That was an accident."

"Leave it out. He was aiming straight at me."

"Listen—you're here to learn—not start a war. I don't have time to teach young tearaways how to behave."

"I'm not a tearaway."

"Then don't act like one. Just concentrate on your tennis. OK?"

Barry nodded. His cheeks were burning, and his throat felt so tight he found it difficult to swallow. There was no way he could convince Hastings that Chetwyn's smash had also been deliberate, so all he'd done was earn himself a black mark. He turned, and walked disconsolately back on to the court.

Lucy watched him with concern. She hadn't seen what happened, but she knew from Barry's expression that he was in trouble. And on the first morning too! Stupid kid, surely he realised how important this week was, that it could open a lot of doors to him? He obviously needed reminding, and she decided to do just that over lunch—if he hadn't been sent home by then!

Sally Brewster had placed boxes in the corners of each service court, and had told the girls to serve fifty balls at each box. Lucy was pleased with her score—twenty hits down the centre line, and twenty-three in the forehand corner. She doubted if many of the others could match that.

When the last girl had completed her hundred serves, Sally clapped her hands for attention. "Right," she announced, "for the next exercise, I want you to play singles with each other diagonally across the court. Twenty-one points with the same girl serving—then twenty-one the other way. If the ball lands the wrong side of the centre line, it's out. So with only half the court to play with, it's vital for the server to gain and hold the net position, and equally vital for the receiver to keep her away from it. Go!"

Lucy found herself playing against Pam Summers, who

won the toss and elected to serve first. It wasn't easy to concentrate, with two other girls playing diagonally across them, but even without any distractions the power of Pam's service made a low, accurate return almost impossible.

Lucy was astonished. There was no hint of the nerves which had plagued poor Pam during their match of the previous summer. She was unerringly accurate, placing each serve within a few inches of the lines, and she used her height so well that the ball sometimes kicked well out of Lucy's reach.

After her twenty-first serve, the two girls approached the net. "If you'd played like that in the County Under-sixteens," said Lucy generously, "you'd 've murdered me."

Pam studied the strings of her racquet. "It's easier when . . ." She stopped abruptly, blushing bright scarlet.

"When what?"

"When mother isn't watching."

"At least she cares! Which is more than mine does."

Sally Brewster called sharply. "Cut the chatter, girls. Get on with it."

Lucy moved back to the baseline and prepared to serve, conscious that her own efforts would look pathetic after Pam's superb display. But she comforted herself with the thought that when it came to match-play there was little to choose between them.

She sat next to Barry at lunch, and asked him several times what had happened that morning. He refused to tell her, but from the way he sat glowering at Chetwyn, sitting diagonally opposite him at the long table, it was obvious where the problem lay.

Chetwyn seemed to be enjoying the situation, taunting Barry like a matador playing a bull. "Pass the salt, would you, old son?" he called cheerfully.

Barry ignored him, so Lucy reached across for the salt.

"Thanks. Your mate didn't seem to understand. Perhaps he calls it the cruet."

Barry put down his knife and fork, his suppressed anger in danger of exploding. "Perhaps you'd like a face full of knuckles."

"Not now thanks," said Chetwyn pleasantly, "I'm eating."

"After dinner, then?"

"Dinner? Don't you mean lunch?"

Barry shot to his feet, and seemed on the point of leaping over the table to get at Chetwyn. A hush fell over the dining-room, as the rest of the group stared curiously at him, waiting tensely for his next move. Lucy noticed that Peter Hastings and Sally Brewster, eating at another table, had looked round to see what had caused the lull in the conversation—so she grabbed Barry's arm and pulled him back into his seat.

"Cool it, Barry," she hissed into his ear, "you're making a fool of yourself."

He remained quite still, staring down at his plate, as everyone relaxed and the conversation resumed.

"I'm afraid he's got a touch of the sulks," said Chetwyn. "I accidentally hit him with a smash this morning, and it doesn't look as if he's forgiven me."

Pam Summers sniffed. "Oh you boys! You're such babies."

"Not at all. He deliberately hit *me*—but I'm not sulking."

After lunch, Lucy and Barry wandered slowly back across the grass towards the Workshop. "You've got to forget Chetwyn," said Lucy. "If you go on like this, they won't invite you again."

Barry picked up a daisy and began to tear the petals off it. "I'd like to smash his face in."

"Why can't you just ignore him?"

"How can I? We have to spend six hours a day together."

"Well, just don't cause any more aggro! We're here for assessment—as people as well as players—and if they decide you're a trouble-maker, you'll be out on your ear. So relax and enjoy yourself."

Barry's muscles still ached from the morning's physical training session. "It's all right for you," he said darkly, "you birds don't have to do them exercises."

But he was wrong. The P.T. instructor was waiting for the girls when they arrived back at the Workshop, and put them through the same agonising routine that the boys had had to endure. Barry watched them gleefully—taking a sadistic delight in their suffering, and in the shrieks of pain that it produced.

Hastings, meanwhile, announced that the afternoon session for the boys would be devoted to the tactics of doubles play. He kept them in the same groups of four, but this time Barry was to partner Chetwyn against Riley and Francis. Barry was relieved; if they were on the same side, Chetwyn wouldn't have an excuse to start anything.

All went well for a set and a half. To Barry's surprise, he and Chetwyn combined perfectly, their greater speed about the court giving them a decisive edge over their opponents. They won the first set six-two, raced into a four-one lead in the second—and it seemed as if the threatening clouds of the morning had rolled away.

But in the sixth game of the second set, they suddenly reappeared. Chetwyn was serving from the right-hand court, with Barry at the net. Riley's return was a good one—hard and flat, down the centre of the court. Barry stretched to cut it off, but his racquet clashed with Chetwyn's, with the result that the ball fell tamely into the bottom of the net.

Barry turned angrily: "That was my ball."

"Rubbish," said Chetwyn, "I had it covered."

"It was my forehand. I could've put it away easy."

"No, Barry," said Hastings, who was leaning against a net-post, "even if you'd reached it, you couldn't 've buried it. And it'd 've taken you too far out of position. They could 've passed you down your backhand."

"But *he* couldn't've buried it either."

"Maybe not—but you'd both have been in your correct positions. The important thing with a good return like that is to keep the ball in play and cover the net. That way, you still have the advantage."

Barry had to admit this made sense. The shot *would* have taken him out of position, leaving an opening down his backhand side which Riley could have exploited. And Chetwyn, following his serve to the net, could obviously have cut off the return while still leaving them both in command of the court.

Chetwyn moved across to the left-hand court, while Barry crouched low at the net, determined to leave no gap down the right-hand tramlines. Something struck him in the small of the back, causing an excruciating pain to ripple outwards from the point of impact.

He whirled round, to see Chetwyn shrugging apologetically. But Barry knew it was no accident—the serve had been deliberately aimed at him. All his pent-up fury suddenly exploded, inflamed by the pain in his back. He didn't care that Hastings was watching; he just wanted to wipe the self-satisfied smile off Chetwyn's face once and for all.

"You sod!" he shouted. Dropping his racquet, he hurled himself at his tormentor, knocking him off his feet. Chetwyn, surprised by the ferocity of the attack, tried to pick himself up—but Barry crashed down on top of him, raining blows at his face and stomach.

He had completely forgotten where he was, and it was only when he felt someone grab him by his shirt collar and haul him to his feet that he began to realise what he'd done.

Hastings was looking down at him grimly. "I warned you, Barry. This is no place for tearaways. Go and pack your bag."

Barry picked up his racquet and started to walk towards the door, conscious that play had stopped on all four courts. Everyone was watching him.

"No!" Lucy detached herself from the girls' group and ran across to Hastings. "Please, Mr Hastings. Give him another chance."

Barry knew she was wasting her time, but he waited for Hastings' reply.

"I gave him another chance. And he blew it."

"But this week—it's so important to him. And I'm sure he's willing to apologise."

"It's too late, Lucy," said Hastings firmly. "We can't afford disruptive influences here. And I'm not interested in kids who'd rather have a punch-up than play tennis."

"But he's not like that ..." Lucy turned and ran over to Barry. "Quick. Go and tell him you're sorry."

"I'm not," said Barry sullenly, "he had it coming."

"But you can't let them send you home—it'd be the end of everything you've worked for. Promise them you won't cause any more bother."

"I can't. 'Cos if he did it again, I'd hang another one on him." And he walked out.

It was a miserable conclusion to a week that had been bright with promise. Lucy was right, he thought dejectedly as he packed his suitcase; it *was* the end of everything he'd worked for. He wondered what Frank would say, how his father would react. They'd never understand the pressure he'd been under; they'd be bound to agree with Hastings that a kid who got involved in punch-ups deserved to be sent home.

He gazed out of the window at the trees, already half-stripped for winter. They, too, were losing everything they had achieved during the summer. But for them, there would be another chance next spring. He doubted whether Barry Grieves would be so lucky.

NINE

His father opened the door and stared at him in astonishment. "I thought you wasn't due back till Saturday."

"I wasn't." Barry squeezed past him into the house, put down his case and hurried into the living-room, hoping to find his mother. But she wasn't there.

His father followed him. "What happened? They run out of money or something?"

"Where's Mum?"

"Working."

"At this time of night?"

"Offices have to be cleaned at this time of night—you should know that by now. I asked you what happened?"

Barry collapsed into a chair. "I got sent home."

"You *what*?" His father looked horrified.

"It wasn't down to me, Dad. There was this bloke—the one who conned me out of me Quarter Final in the County Under-sixteens . . ."

"Not down to you, eh? Then how come it was you that got sent home?"

Barry avoided his eye. "Cos I thumped him," he said sheepishly.

"Thumped him? Why?"

"He started to needle me soon as I got there. And he served straight into me back."

"Did they give *him* his marching orders?"

"No. They thought it was an accident, see? Only I knew different."

His father walked slowly over to Barry's chair and towered menacingly over him. "You're the one that ought to get a thumping, Barry. I go crawling to the Headmaster to give you a week off school—and you're back after twenty-four hours. What am I going to tell him?"

Barry had considered this problem on the bus, and had come up with a possible solution. "Don't tell him nothing," he said.

"Eh?"

"I needn't go back till Monday. If I stayed away the rest of the week, I could pretend I'd finished the course."

His father moved away to the mantelpiece, and stood with his back to the room. "You're a disgrace," he said bitterly. "That's what you are. A bleedin' disgrace."

"They had it in for me right from the start, Dad! I didn't stand a chance."

This seemed to strike a responsive chord. His father turned to face him, his bitterness now directed at the faceless powers-that-be who had treated his son so unfairly. "Well don't say I didn't warn you! If you step out of your class, you're asking for trouble . . ."

The doorbell rang. Barry stayed slumped in his chair while his father went to answer it. But he sat up straight when he heard Frank's voice. His stomach felt as if someone was tying knots in it; he hadn't reckoned on having to face the coach so soon.

Frank appeared in the doorway, tight-lipped and stern. "Well? What've you got to say for yourself?"

Barry shifted uncomfortably. "How d'you find out?"

"Peter Hastings rang me."

"Oh." To Barry's embarrassment, his eyes started to fill

with tears. It was years since he'd cried, and the choking sensation took him completely by surprise. But he suddenly found he couldn't keep his frustration and disappointment bottled up any longer; he put his head in his hands and wept uncontrollably.

"It was that Chetwyn," he blurted between sobs, "he kept on at me. I just couldn't help meself."

"Bleedin' snobs," said his father indignantly. "That kid he thumped—I'll bet he had it coming."

Frank sat on the arm of Barry's chair. "Taught you a lesson, has it? About self-control?"

"Yeh."

"Good. Because things aren't quite as bad as you think."

Barry wiped his eyes with his sleeve and blinked up at him. "Eh?"

"I told Peter Hastings there were some extenuating circumstances which might explain—if not excuse—your behaviour. He knows all about Chetwyn, and he agrees he might have been a bit hasty. So, if you promise not to cause any more trouble, he's willing to let you go back and finish the course."

"Go back? Face all them kids after what happened today? I couldn't. I just couldn't."

"You'd rather face 'em at school?"

"I could keep me head down till Monday. Work out at the Club. Nobody from school goes there."

"That's up to your father."

Barry glanced at him anxiously. "Well, Dad?"

His father bit his lip thoughtfully, then shrugged. "If you went back now, you'd be making right twits of both of us. Only if the Headmaster gets to hear you're playing truant, I don't know nothing about it, OK?"

So it was agreed that Barry should practise at the Club for

the rest of the week. But when he arrived there the next day, he found he still hadn't fully atoned for his sins.

Major Houghton called to him as he opened the gate to the courts. "Grieves?" He waited as the Major hurried up to him. "I'm afraid we've cancelled your membership."

Barry could hardly believe his ears. "Eh?"

"We heard what happened at Bisham Abbey. And we're not prepared to give free places to young hooligans."

"Now hold on a minute, Major . . ."

"I told you when Frank Abbott first brought you to me. In return for our patronage, we expect you to behave yourself—not to bring discredit on the Club . . ."

"But they're willing to take me back."

"Well we're not," said the Major curtly. "I'm sorry—but you're no longer welcome here." And he marched briskly back to the pavilion.

Barry opened his mouth to protest, but, realising it would be useless, turned and walked slowly back towards the car park. Tears pricked his eyes again; they'd made up their minds without hearing his side of the story. Well, there was nothing he could do about it; he certainly wasn't going to go down on his bended knees to them. The old man had been right—they *were* a bunch of snobs.

He went straight round to Frank's flat and told him that the Major had given him the Big E. Frank was furious, but said there was nothing he could do about it; it was a private Club, and the Committee had a right to accept or reject a member as it saw fit. However, he was not without influence in the tennis world, and now Barry was out in the cold, promised to use it on his behalf.

Next morning, he was waiting in his car outside Mr Ferris's shop when Barry returned from his paper round.

"What's this?" asked Barry, leaning in through the window. "Free Minicab service?"

"Get in," Frank told him, "I'm taking you to meet someone."

"Who?"

"Another of my pupils."

"Why?"

"'Cos he wants to meet *you*. That's why."

Barry climbed into the passenger seat, and they drove into the City. He'd only been there once before, on his way to the Tower, but he recognised many of the buildings from a book called *London Landmarks* which his Aunt Winnie had given him for his tenth birthday . . . the Mansion House, the Bank of England, the Guildhall . . .

He wondered who this mysterious pupil was, and why he wanted to meet him. But Frank refused to answer any of his questions, saying only that it was just possible he might hear something to his advantage.

They turned into an underground car-park below a multi-storied office block, and travelled up in the lift to the fourteenth floor. There, they passed through a glass door with the words BOUSFIELD & CO. LTD printed on it in gold.

A smartly-dressed young secretary ushered them into a large office overlooking the Thames, where a stout, grey-haired man with thick horn-rimmed glasses rose from his desk to greet them.

Frank turned to Barry. "This is Mr Bousfield."

Bousfield walked round his desk and offered his hand. "Hello, young man."

Barry stared at him. The face seemed familiar, and he searched his memory for a clue. Then it came to him. He was the man who'd stood watching from the next court while he and Frank had their first knock-up.

He took the hand. "I seen you before, right? You was with Frank when he first sussed me out?"

Bousfield's eyes were enormous behind the thick lenses.

"That's right. I hear you've come a long way since then."

"Yeh. He's taught me a lot."

"But not how to control your temper?"

Barry glanced at Frank, irritated at being talked about behind his back. "Been grassing on me, eh? Out of order, that."

Bousfield took off his glasses and began to polish them with a spotless handkerchief. "Learned your lesson, have you?"

"What do you care?" Barry had had enough lectures lately, and he wasn't going to take another from a complete stranger.

"Answer the question, Barry," said Frank sharply.

He didn't see why he should, but as it seemed to be important, he made an effort to control his temper. "Dunno," he said gruffly, looking down at his feet, "maybe I have."

"I hope so." Bousfield replaced his glasses and leaned back against his desk. "Because Frank tells me you need sponsorship—someone to pay your expenses for the next few years. But no one's going to sponsor a wild kid who's handier with his fists than a racquet."

Barry frowned. "You work for a sports firm or something?"

"No. If I decide to back you, it'd be a private deal. Between you and me."

"Why would you want to back me?"

"Because I'm a tennis freak. And because I trust Frank's judgement."

Barry glanced at Frank. "This is down to you, is it?"

"I told Mr Bousfield you were a long shot," said Frank, smiling, "but you might be worth a bit of a flutter."

"You'll have to show me some form, of course." Bousfield moved back behind his desk. "I want to be sure you're broken in."

"Show you some form? When?"

Bousfield raised his eyebrows at Frank, who moved to the window and stood looking down at the river. "Next Easter. The first big Junior Tournament of the year. It's for Under-eighteens, so you probably won't get very far—but it'll be good experience for you ..."

"And it'll give me a chance to look you over," added Bousfield.

Barry's spirits rose. He was no longer out in the cold. "OK," he said softly.

Frank turned away from the window. "This could be your last chance, Barry. So no blow-ups, eh?"

"Me, coach? Got the wrong feller, haven't you? They've just been on at me to take over as Archbishop of Canterbury."

"No one's expecting you to be an archbishop." Bousfield leaned back in his chair and swivelled it gently from side to side. "Because archbishops don't win tennis matches."

"I shouldn't worry," said Frank drily, "Canterbury's safe for some time yet."

On the way home, he told Barry that he intended to work him really hard through the winter. They had five months to prepare for the Easter Tournament—time enough for Barry to build up his stamina and knock some of the rough edges off his game.

With something definite to aim for, Barry began to push himself to the limit, following Frank's punishing training programme to the letter and chasing round the court with renewed energy and enthusiasm. He used his paper round as a check on his physical condition, trying each day to break his previous record. This caused several more mix-ups with the papers, but Mr Ferris didn't seem to mind too much; rumours of Barry's prowess at tennis had begun to spread through the neighbourhood, so the newsagent, like many of his customers, understood why he took his paper round at such breakneck speed.

Now he was no longer a member of the Club, he had to use the public courts. But it didn't matter; all he needed was a court and a practice-wall, and the fact that the facilities were shabbier than those at the Club was more than balanced by a sense of freedom, with no Major Houghton to hassle him.

When he returned to school, he was relieved to discover that no one seemed to have heard of his disgrace at Bisham Abbey. For once, he was grateful for the general lack of interest in tennis; the game's grapevine didn't extend to this part of North London. The Headmaster, passing him in a corridor, asked how he'd got on, and seemed satisfied with Barry's non-committal reply.

One afternoon, two weeks after his interview with Bousfield, he arrived home to find Lucy sitting in the living-room with his mother. A tea-tray lay on the table between them, and they behaved as if they'd known each other for years.

Lucy greeted him with a bright smile. "Hi."

He frowned at her suspiciously. "What're you doing here?"

"You didn't come to see me. So I came to see you."

"Why?"

His mother broke in, uncharacteristically severe. "What d'you mean—why? Where's your manners, Barry? A nice girl goes to all this trouble to look you up . . ."

"Nice girl?" He looked round the room in mock puzzlement. "I don't see no nice girl. All I see is a scrubber."

His mother patted her hair in embarrassment. "I don't know why you bother with him, Lucy—I really don't!"

"Neither do I," said Lucy. "It's certainly not his charm, that's for sure."

"Another piece of cake, dear?"

"No, thanks. I have to watch my weight."

"Well *I* don't," said Barry. He leaned across Lucy,

grabbed a large piece of cake and stuffed it into his mouth.

His mother shrugged helplessly. "See what I mean? No manners!"

"He can't be *your* son, Mrs Grieves." Lucy sounded genuinely concerned. "You sure he isn't a changeling or something?"

"Could be. Come to think of it, I was in the next bed to an M.P.'s wife at the Maternity Hospital. You reckon they switched babies?"

"Oh, shut up, Mum." The way they were talking about him as if he wasn't there made Barry uncomfortable. He turned to Lucy. "You just here to put the boot in, or what?"

She looked hurt. "Aren't you pleased to see me?"

"Yeh. Sort of."

"Only sort of? After all I've given up for you?"

He couldn't think what she was talking about. "Given up?"

"I've resigned from the Club."

"Eh?"

"That pompous Major told me they'd thrown you out—because you'd got sent home from Bisham. So I blew my top. Told him what he could do with himself—and his membership."

Barry stared at her in amazement. She really was an incredible person. To go out on a limb for him like that, to tell the Major he could stuff his membership—it was the sort of thing people only did in books.

"You didn't have to do that," he said gruffly.

His mother refilled Lucy's cup. "Course she didn't. She still did it though. You got a real mate here, Barry."

"Yeh."

"So now we both need somewhere to play," said Lucy. "And what I came to ask was—if I joined another club, would the great Barry Grieves do me the honour of practising with me? As my guest?"

He grinned. "Fancy some more free lessons, do you?"

Before she could reply, his father appeared in the doorway, carrying an evening paper. He blinked at Lucy. "Hello. Who's this, then?"

"Lucy Roberts, Dad," Barry told him. Then, to Lucy, "Me old man."

She stood up, still holding her tea-cup, and offered her hand. "Nice to meet you, Mr Grieves," she said politely.

He walked forwards to shake hands, bemused by the unaccustomed formality. "Likewise, I'm sure."

Lucy put down her cup. "Well, I must be going. Thanks for the tea, Mrs Grieves."

"You're welcome, dear. Come and see us again, eh?"

"I will." Lucy moved to the door, then turned back. "You're entering for the Easter Under-eighteens, Barry?"

"Yeh."

"The sooner we get another club the better, then. I'll be in touch."

She disappeared into the passage. Barry's father waited till he heard the front door open and close, then sat down and unfolded his paper. "Bit la-di-da, isn't she? What'd she want?"

"Nothing," said Barry. "she's doing me a favour."

"That's why we got the cake out, is it?" Then, pointing an accusing finger at his wife, "I thought you was saving it for the weekend."

"I was. But I couldn't just give her bread and jam, could I?"

"Why not? *We* have to make do with it." The finger was suddenly directed at Barry. "And what's all this about an Easter Tournament?"

Barry, who had wanted to give his parents a chance to

forget about tennis for a while, hadn't mentioned either the Tournament or his visit to Bousfield's office. But now the cat was well and truly out of the bag, and he wasn't sure which way it would jump.

"Frank wants me to play, Dad," he explained soothingly. "There's a bloke who's thinking of sponsoring me, and it's a chance for him to suss me out."

"Bloke? What bloke?"

"Some business geezer. If I do OK, he'll pay me expenses for the next three years."

His father's finger wagged threateningly. "You're not going to miss any more school . . ."

"Don't need to. It's during the Easter holidays."

His father regarded him thoughtfully. "Maybe I'll come and suss you out an' all."

"You?"

"I never seen you play a match, have I? Seems to me Frank's been making all the decisions around here—and it's about time *I* made one."

This didn't sound too good. "What d'you mean?" asked Barry apprehensively.

"I mean, if I don't reckon there's any future in this tennis lark, I'm going to put a stop to it once and for all. Now how about some of that cake, eh?"

He leaned forward to take a piece of cake, bit into it with a satisfied grunt and settled back to read his paper.

Barry glanced at his mother, who smiled encouragingly back at him. She was obviously pleased that his father was coming to watch him, and completely unaware of the added pressure which Barry would have to endure. But it made the Easter Tournament even more important. If he didn't do well, he would not only lose a sponsor, but his father might carry out his threat to "put a stop to it once and for all". He was uneasily conscious of having blown every chance that had come his way so far: If he blew it this time, it really would be the end.

*

Wendy was curled up on the sofa, watching television. "Look at that girl!" she shouted disgustedly as Lucy entered. "Can't act her way out of a paper bag!"

Lucy slumped into a chair and watched for a while. The object of her sister's derision seemed to her to be a perfectly adequate actress; a little over the top, perhaps, but then it was supposed to be a comedy. And the studio audience were falling about. "I think she's rather good," she said.

Wendy snorted: "You would!"

"What's the matter with her?"

"Well, for a start, she's supposed to be cockney, right? But she's obviously never been within a hundred miles of Bow Bells."

"You could do better, I suppose?"

"Matter of fact, I could, dearie."

Lucy thought her accent embarrassingly bad. "That's not real cockney. That's stage cockney."

"What do you know about it?"

"I had tea with a cockney family today."

"Oh really? Who?" Lucy turned with a start. She hadn't heard her mother enter the room.

"Barry Grieves' parents."

"The boy there was all that fuss about at the Club? You're not still chasing after him, are you?"

"I'm not chasing after him, Mother," said Lucy irritably. "He's a friend, that's all. And after the way they treated him, he needs all the friends he can get."

Her mother crossed over to the television and switched it off. "I still think you over-reacted. You could've registered your protest without resigning."

"They wouldn't 've listened to me. Juniors have to be seen but not heard at that Club. All they're interested in are the geriatrics."

"Then why resign?" asked Wendy, swinging herself up into a sitting position. "What difference will it make?"

"I just had to do something. Major Houghton was so unfair."

Mrs Roberts started to rearrange a vase of flowers. "But look at it from his point of view. The boy was sent home from Bisham Abbey in disgrace."

Lucy sighed impatiently. "I've explained all that, Mother. It wasn't Barry's fault."

"No," said Wendy drily, "of course not."

"What's that supposed to mean?"

"You make it very obvious, Beetle. You've hardly talked about anything else since you came back. Got a crush on him, haven't you?"

"Crush on who? Or rather—whom?" a deep voice called from the hall.

Lucy's heart jumped, as it always did when her father came home. He appeared in the doorway, tall and distinguished-looking, dressed in a smart pin-striped suit and carrying a briefcase. "Evening, all."

"Hello, darling." Lucy's mother gave him a peck on the cheek. "Drink?"

"Thanks." He put down his briefcase and sat on the edge of Lucy's chair. "So. Love is in the air, is it? Who's the lucky man, Lucy?"

"Oh, don't listen to Wendy, Daddy! Ever since they cast her as Juliet, she's started seeing Romeos all over the place."

"False alarm, eh? Pity." He kissed Lucy on the top of her head and stood up again. "I thought for one glorious moment you might've found someone to take you off my hands. Then there'd have been one less hotel room to pay for."

Wendy frowned. "Hotel room? What on earth are you talking about, Daddy?"

"I've decided to take two weeks' holiday at Easter. So I thought we might all pop over to France."

"France!" Wendy jumped to her feet excitedly. "That'll be great."

"But . . ." Lucy bit her lip, aware that she was about to sound like a wet blanket.

Her father stared down at her. "But what?"

"I'm playing in the Under-eighteen Tournament at Easter."

"Oh! I'd forgotten about that."

He looked very disappointed, and Lucy quickly tried to make amends. "You go. I can manage on my own."

Her mother handed her father a glass. "Nonsense, darling. Besides, we promised to come and watch you."

"I don't mind. I don't want to spoil your holiday."

"No," said her father, "a promise is a promise. Perhaps we can go down to the coast for a few days instead."

But this didn't appease Wendy. "You don't *have* to play in this Tournament, do you, Beetle?" she demanded crossly. "I mean it wouldn't be the end of the world if you missed one, would it?"

"I'm sorry—it's important. If I'm going to improve my ranking this year . . ." Lucy trailed off miserably, conscious that to people outside the tennis world her position in the National Rankings was supremely unimportant.

"Well never mind," said her father cheerfully. "Perhaps we can go over to France in the summer."

"No, we can't." Wendy was still furious. "Because there'll be some other grotty tournament then! There always is." She flounced out of the room.

Lucy felt like a killjoy. She didn't blame Wendy for being

annoyed; she herself would have been choked if they'd had to cancel a holiday because of one of her sister's first nights. And though her parents hadn't tried to make her change her mind, she knew that they too didn't really understand. To them, one tournament was very like another. And Wendy was right; in the summer, there would be more "grotty tournaments".

Only they weren't grotty—they were all desperately important. There were always new girls coming up, and if you didn't play the whole of the Junior Circuit, you could easily find yourself off the ranking list altogether. And that could mean having to drop out of the elite training squads. Which in turn could mean falling further and further behind her rivals.

No, she had only two choices—to compete in every event, or to resign herself to gradual oblivion. She wasn't good enough to pick and choose. Very soon now, she would have to decide whether or not to chuck it all in . . .

TEN

Lucy joined another club, and all through the winter she and Barry practised hard. Besides following the gruelling training programme prescribed by Frank, they spent long hours on court, unselfishly pointing out gaps in each other's defences, and advising on how to plug them.

On weekdays they usually had the Club to themselves, as most of the other members were office workers who didn't arrive home till after dark. Even at weekends, there were nearly always some free courts: only a handful of hardy souls braved the frosty mornings for an hour or two, before scurrying back to their burrows to thaw out.

But Barry and Lucy didn't notice the cold. They both had the Easter Tournament fixed firmly in their sights, and they planned their campaigns with military precision, aiming to bring themselves to peak form and fitness by the middle of March.

For the first time since Frank took him under his wing, Barry felt no outside pressure. His father seemed content to wait till the Under-eighteen Championship before delivering his judgement—and there was no Chetwyn or Major Houghton to get under his skin. So he was able to concentrate on his game.

One thing bothered him however. Good as Lucy was, she wasn't the ideal sparring partner; she just didn't have the power to stretch him, the power that his male opponents would certainly possess. He knew he needed someone stronger to practise with, and Lucy also seemed aware of the problem; but when she suggested that he find someone else, he told her he was quite happy. *He* was certainly the ideal sparring partner for *her*, and he was glad of the chance to pay her back for all her encouragement and support.

Besides, he still had his lessons. Because of Frank's other commitments, these were reduced to three a week during the winter—but Barry looked forward to them enormously. He was constantly amazed at how much there was to learn about an apparently simple game.

He began to learn about the tactics and psychology of match-play. He had always supposed that you went on to the court, played your best—and if your best was good enough, you won. But there was far more to winning than that. Frank taught him to look for weaknesses in his opponent's game during the knock up ... to exploit those weaknesses for a while, and then, when the opponent seemed to be finding his touch, to switch to the other wing ... and to play percentage tennis on the important points.

"Use your head," Frank kept saying. "You can often beat a better player by out-smarting him." So Barry, who had always been absorbed in his own game, began to watch Frank, noticing how he preferred to half-volley the ball rather than move his feet. He found that by driving deep to the baseline he could force a weak return, which he could usually put away by coming in quickly to the net. And for the first time since they started playing together, he began to take sets off the coach.

In early January, the shale courts at the club became unplayable. But Frank, who seemed to know everyone in the tennis world, arranged for Barry and Lucy to use an indoor court in St John's Wood for an hour every afternoon. The hiring charges, according to the notice outside the court, were astronomical, and they hoped Frank wasn't paying for it out of his own pocket. But when Lucy offered to ask her father for the money, the coach told her it wasn't costing him anything. The manager of the court owed him a favour.

As Easter approached, Barry grew more and more nervous. With so much riding on the tournament, he wondered if he would be able to do himself justice. Frank and Lucy told him not to worry, to forget about the spectators and concentrate on his opponent—but it wasn't easy. He lay awake at night, picturing himself muffing shot after shot, with Bousfield sadly shaking his head, and his father turning away in disgust.

His sense of foreboding increased when Frank told him he'd been drawn against Ken Maddox, the National Under-eighteen Champion and number one seed. Lucy, however, saw this as a stroke of good luck. He wasn't expected to win—so he had nothing to lose. If he played his natural game, no one could be disappointed. But it was a big "if", thought Barry gloomily; he wondered how McEnroe and Borg could play so well with fifteen thousand people round the court and millions more watching on television. His own knees turned to jelly at the thought of the handful of spectators who would turn up to see Maddox wipe him off the court.

The only consolation was the prospect of actually playing at Wimbledon! Not on the grass courts, where the most famous tournament in the world was held at the end of June, but on shale. It didn't matter though; the very name was magic. And even if he never picked up a tennis racquet again, he could always say he'd played there. It was a memory he'd cherish as long as he lived.

The great day finally dawned, and Frank drove Barry and his parents down to South London. As they passed through the gates of the All England Club, Barry's heart missed a beat. There were the ivy-clad walls of the centre court which he'd seen so often on television, there was the scoreboard which had relayed the progress of so many heroic struggles to the spectators outside, and there were the outside courts, unlined and netless, where so many big fish had been humbled by unknown minnows.

His mother seemed equally impressed. She stood by Frank's car, staring up at the towering walls and saying, "Well I never!" every few seconds, saucer-eyed with wonder. His father, however, was determined not to be over-awed. "Smaller than I thought," he said dismissively. "Looks much bigger on the box."

There was no sign of Lucy, who was driving down with her parents, and Barry suggested they go and look for her. But there was no time; they hadn't walked more than a few steps before there was an announcement over the Tannoy: "Maddox and Grieves—Court One, please. Maddox and Grieves—Court One."

Barry grinned. "Pity it's not the big one. I could've had a few thousand punters watching me."

"Some day perhaps," Frank told him. "Anyway, you're on the main hard court, so on your bike! And good luck."

Ken Maddox turned out to be a young blond giant, well over six feet tall and built like Superman. Barry's heart sank; it was going to be even more one-sided than he thought. There was no chance of *this* big fish being humbled by a minnow.

Unlike Chetwyn, however, he was pleasant and friendly. "Hi," he said, as Barry joined him at the entrance to the court. "Don't play too well, will you! My sponsor's watching."

"So's mine." This was stretching the truth a bit because Bousfield hadn't turned up yet, nor was there any definite sponsorship deal, but Barry didn't want Maddox to think he was rubbish. If his opponent was nervous too, then so much the better; as far as he was concerned, Barry was an unknown quantity, so the casual mention of a sponsor might undermine his confidence a little.

There was no sign of nerves during the knock-up. Barry searched in vain for some sign of weakness, but Maddox seemed to play every shot with equal crispness and power. And his service was devastating—faster than anything Barry had met before, and disguised so beautifully that it was impossible to anticipate its direction.

As Maddox had won the toss, Barry had no choice but to face this fearsome weapon in the very first game. He crouched low near the service line, a swarm of butterflies flapping around inside his stomach.

Behind him, he heard his mother's hoarse whisper: "It's not fair! That lad's much older than our Barry."

His father's reply was just as audible: "You got to expect it, love. He's stepping up a division."

"Well, I still don't think it's fair. What chance has he got against that big lout?"

Suddenly and unexpectedly, the butterflies left Barry's stomach. If that's what they all thought, then Lucy was right—he had nothing to lose. The odds were heavily against him, but he determined to fight every inch of the way. Maddox might emerge the winner, but he was going to have to earn his victory!

The first serve came crashing down, swinging away to the forehand. Barry lunged desperately at the ball, managed to catch it on the end of his racquet and sent it screaming back down the line. An unplayable return! Behind him, Barry heard someone clap, and knew without turning round that it was his mother.

Maddox frowned, crossed over to the left-hand court and

served again. Barry, gambling on the backhand, guessed right. He was already in position by the time the ball reached him, leaned into it and arrowed it past his opponent's forehand before he could move.

The next two serves were slower, giving Maddox time to follow them up to the net. But Barry swiped them both cross-court—and Maddox, anticipating more drives down the line, couldn't get his racquet to either of them.

It was too good to be true, thought Barry, as he crossed over at the end of the game. To take the blond giant's first serve to love! That probably didn't happen very often, and it must've shaken him a bit. The important thing now was to keep him on the defensive by holding his own serve . . .

Frank, meanwhile, having seen Bousfield's Jaguar drive through the gates, was waiting on the concourse for him.

"Sorry I'm late, Frank," said Bousfield, as he reappeared from the car-park. "Important client dropped in just as I was leaving."

"It's OK, Mr Bousfield," Frank reassured him. "Barry's match has just started. He's on Court One."

"Court One? Star attraction, eh?"

"His opponent is. He's the Number One seed."

On the way to the court, Frank explained that there was a three-year difference between the players, and that in terms of experience the gap was even wider. So Barry was on a hiding to nothing.

Bousfield listened with amusement. "I'm sure he doesn't need you to make excuses for him," he said, smiling. "And don't worry. I'm not expecting miracles from a kid of fourteen."

"Fifteen. He's had a birthday since you saw him last."

Frank introduced Bousfield to Barry's parents, who couldn't wait to tell him the score. "Barry's leading three-one," said Mrs Grieves proudly. "You'd never think it, would you? I mean, look at the difference in sizes."

"Yes," said Bousfield, as Maddox served a sizzling ace down the centre line. "A David and Goliath confrontation. But remember who won *that* battle!"

Maddox won his serve, bringing the score to three-two in Barry's favour. There then followed a titanic game, involving twelve deuces, with both competitors playing at the top of their form. Frank tried to hide his tension: he knew that this could well prove to be the turning point of the match. There was a superstition in tennis that the seventh game was vital, but the sixth was often even more so. The difference between four-two and three-all was of great psychological importance, with the loser having to make up a two-game deficit instead of starting the next game on even terms.

For ten minutes the match was balanced on a knife-edge, with one player gaining the advantage point, only to be pulled back to deuce by the other. The tennis was spectacular; Barry, no longer plagued by butterflies, was countering Maddox's greater power with his own tremendous speed about the court—and the ball flew backwards and forwards across the net at seemingly impossible angles.

Mr Grieves' jaw sagged lower and lower, weighed down with astonishment. "Blimey," he said softly, "I never realised that Barry . . ."

"Realised what?" asked his wife.

"That he was this good."

"Frank did. He told us he was special."

Mr Grieves looked thoughtful. "He doesn't need Frank. A kid with his natural talent—all he needs is someone to look after his training. And I could do that."

"You don't know nothing about tennis, Jack. Leave it to Frank—he's the professional."

"Listen." Just out of Frank's earshot, Mr Grieves spoke out

of the side of his mouth, "The reason Frank's sniffing round our Barry is 'cos he smells money. Big money. And if he's right, I don't see why we shouldn't keep it in the family . . ."

At that moment, possibly as a punishment for his father's greed, fate decided that Barry should lose the game. His delicate stop-volley trembled for an agonising moment on the top of the net, then fell back. It had been a particularly exhausting rally, and both players bent double, desperately sucking air into their empty lungs.

Bousfield shook his head in sympathy. "Bad luck, that. It could just as easily have fallen the other way."

"Yes," Frank agreed, "but it'll be a test of Barry's character. Now we'll really find out what he's made of."

*

Two hundred metres away, on Court Fifteen, Lucy was also in the middle of her first-round match. She had been drawn against Claire Sugden, a raw, inexperienced player from Yorkshire, competing in her first major tournament—and so far the contest had been completely one-sided. Lucy had swept through the first set without losing a game, and had just held her service to take a two-one lead in the second.

But despite the score, she was becoming more and more irritated. Her father, sitting next to her mother by the side of the court, seemed to have lost all interest in the match; after the first game, he had taken out a financial newspaper which he had been reading ever since. Lucy felt hurt and resentful; he'd been too busy to come and see her play for nearly a year, and she'd been looking forward to showing him how much she had improved. This match was the ideal opportunity, as her opponent didn't seem able to get her game together and presented no threat; but her father was obviously bored to death. He hadn't looked up from the paper for the last quarter of an hour.

Mrs Roberts, huddled in her thickest coat, caught the angry glare Lucy gave her father during the change-over. She jabbed him in the ribs with her elbow. "Put that away, George. Now you're here, you might show some interest."

Mr Roberts looked up, startled. "Sorry." He folded his paper. "What's the score?"

"Two-one to Lucy. And she won the first set six-love."

"Looks like she's got it sewn up, then. I wonder if the bar's open?"

"Can't you wait till the end of the match?"

Mr Roberts shivered. "No. It's freezing out here. If I don't have a large whisky immediately, I shall turn into an iceberg." He stood up and walked briskly away towards the concourse.

Out of the corner of her eye, Lucy saw her father leave the side of the court. Where on earth was he going now? To get another paper? If watching her was such a drag, she wondered why he'd bothered to come at all. Perhaps this was his way of paying her back for making him miss his holiday in France.

She suddenly realised she was fifteen-forty down. She really must concentrate! It wouldn't be a disaster if she lost this game, because she was confident she had Claire's measure, but she never liked to give easy points away. Yet that's just what she'd done by not giving the match her full attention, sending her last two returns—shots which she knew she should have turned into winners—tamely into the net.

So she concentrated. But Claire's next serve hit the line, and the tape took all the pace off the ball. Lucy was already committed to the shot, and though she desperately tried to readjust, she was too early. Her return was consequently much too high, falling three or four metres beyond the baseline.

She stamped her foot in annoyance. The last point was just bad luck, but if she hadn't allowed her mind to wander she'd never have got into a fifteen-forty position in the first place. It was sheer carelessness, she told herself, unnecessary and unforgivable—and there must be no more lapses of concentration. She must finish off the match as quickly and efficiently as possible.

But her opponent was now in no mood to be finished off. Encouraged by winning the fourth game, to level the set at two games all, Claire suddenly began to play inspired tennis. It was as if she realised the tide had turned, and that she had a real chance of taking the match.

Her luck changed too. All the net-cords and bad bounces were in her favour, while Lucy's shots seemed to catch mysterious little gusts of wind which carried them centimetres outside the lines. She gritted her teeth, knowing that bad and good luck usually evened itself out over a whole match. But to her growing dismay, the tide showed no sign of turning; try as she might, she couldn't seem to force it back. It was as if an invisible gremlin was sitting on her shoulder, willing her opponent's shots to go in, and her own to go out.

The next four games slipped away, and she lost the set six-two. Towelling herself down, she suddenly remembered her match with Pam Summers nine months ago. That day, after she had levelled at set-all, she had known she was going to win. Now she was on the receiving end, she knew with equal certainty that she was going to lose.

It wasn't that she was giving up; she'd fight till the last point. But she sensed an irresistible force that was running against her; and if that force had decided that she was going to lose, there was nothing she could do about it.

It had all started with her father, of course. Burying his head in his paper, then walking away like that—no wonder fate had decided she wasn't worth supporting. If one's own family didn't care, what was the point? Her mother was still there, of course, but she looked bored stiff too. She was probably worrying more about the length of her skirt than the score.

She walked back to begin the final set—and promptly served a double fault. Usually, such a mistake would gee her up, make her even more determined to win the next point, but this time she took it as confirmation of what she already knew—that this was just not her day.

Tired and listless, she lost her opening service game ... then Claire's serve ... then her own again. She was doing little more than keeping the ball in play, waiting for some sign that the tide was turning, but knowing it was a forlorn hope.

Her father returned as they were changing over at the end of the third game. He was carrying two paper cups, one of which he raised at Lucy, giving her an encouraging wink.

Lucy stared back at him stonily. So that's where he'd been! A visit to the bar, it seemed, was more important than watching his daughter play tennis. Well, it didn't matter now—the damage was done. She just wished he *had* gone to France, and taken the rest of the family with him!

As she walked dejectedly back to the baseline, her father sat down next to her mother and handed her one of the paper cups. "Here. Brought you a snifter."

Mrs Roberts accepted it gratefully. "Thanks. I think I'm suffering from frostbite."

"How's she doing now?"

"Not so good. She's lost the second set, and she's three down in the third."

"Thought she looked a bit down in the dumps." Mr Roberts sipped his drink. "Maybe we'll get our trip to France after all."

The rest of the match was a formality. Lucy surprised

herself by winning her remaining service games, but Claire easily held her own serve, taking the final set six-two.

As they shook hands, Lucy wondered why she felt so detached. Claire's face, flushed with pleasure, was a reflection of the way she herself must have looked after her victory over Pam the previous summer. Well, good luck to her! You win some, you lose some. Swings and roundabouts. It was strange how little she cared.

"Bad luck, darling," said her mother cheerfully, as she came off the court.

"Yes, bad luck, old thing," echoed her father. "I thought you played jolly well."

Lucy rounded on him, her bitterness suddenly overflowing. "How would you know? You were in the bar most of the time."

She had the satisfaction of seeing him glance guiltily at her mother.

*

Barry's game was beginning to crack up. He had put up a tremendous fight, and the match had been a cliff-hanger all the way; but now, having lost the first set by a whisker, he was three-four down in the second—and under increasing pressure. He had to win his service to level at four-all, but Maddox's returns were becoming faster and deeper all the time, allowing him almost total domination of the net.

Barry, realising how important it was to get his first serve in, had resorted to spin for greater accuracy. But for some reason his left wrist seemed to have acquired a will of its own, and he couldn't throw the ball up straight.

Frank had taught him not to hit the ball if his throw-up wasn't correct, but there was a limit to the amount of times you could go through the motions of serving and then apologise to your opponent for a false alarm. So Barry was forced to hit the ball no matter how badly he threw it up, with the result that he could get no spin on it, presenting Maddox with an easy return and free access to the net position.

And this wasn't the only problem. Maddox's greater weight of shot gave Barry no time to get into the correct position for his backhand, which was becoming more and more erratic. Conscious that if he didn't go for a clean winner Maddox would have an easy volley down the forehand, he had started to overhit—and his opponent, sensing a weakness, was exploiting it mercilessly.

But he fought on, using well-disguised topspin lobs to keep Maddox away from the net, and managed to reach game point. This, however, proved to be the end of his resistance. Three deep returns to the backhand from Maddox, three overhit drives from Barry, and the game was lost. Then four powerful serves from Maddox, and the match was lost.

Barry was surprised by the volume of applause from the spectators as he ran to the net to shake hands. It wasn't just his mother; everyone was clapping with genuine enthusiasm. And Maddox was generous with his praise. "You were great, kid," he said ruefully. "I had to play out of my skin to beat you."

Outside the court, Bousfield and Frank were waiting for him. Bousfield offered his hand. "Fine match, Barry. Congratulations."

Barry, who had never expected to be congratulated on a defeat, began to realise that he had scored some sort of victory. "Thanks," he said, grinning.

"About my offer. We've got a deal—OK?"

"T'rrific."

"Frank'll bring you up to my office next week, and we'll work out the details. Arrange it with my secretary, eh, Frank?"

"Right," said Frank.

Bousfield moved away as Barry's parents appeared. "Well played, love." His mother kissed him on the cheek. "Not fair, was it? Putting you up against a lad as big as that?"

"I could've won, Mum," Barry told her, "I know I could. Next time, I'll keep him away from the net . . ."

"There's not going to be a next time, Barry," said Frank quietly. "Not for quite a while."

Barry stared at him in astonishment. "Eh?"

"You're not playing any more tournaments till we've sorted a few things out."

"Such as?"

"Your service and your backhand. They've both got to be taken to pieces and reassembled."

"No, they haven't," said Barry's father unexpectedly, "you can leave him to me now."

Frank frowned. "You?"

"We're grateful for all you've done, Frank, but we don't need you no more. *I'm* taking over."

"Taking over?"

"As Barry's coach. I can see what's wrong just as well as you."

"No, you can't. I don't mean to be rude, Mr Grieves—but even if you *could* spot his faults, you wouldn't know how to put them right."

"There's no big deal about it. All you need's a bit of common sense!"

"You need more than that, Dad." Barry was beginning to feel uneasy. "You need to've been a player . . ."

"Rubbish! I've seen enough tennis on the box to know what's what."

"That's ridiculous," said Frank angrily. "You think you can teach someone to sing just by watching a few operas?"

"I don't watch operas. But I'll tell you this—I'll bet there's a lot less to it than the singing teachers make out."

"You're making a big mistake. Amateur coaches can do a lot of harm."

"Well, you have to say that, don't you? To protect your job."

This was monstrously unfair, and Barry thought it was time he came to Frank's defence. "Don't be funny, Dad. I'd never've got anywhere without Frank."

"Course you would. Maybe not as fast, but you'd've made it all right. Natural talent—that's what you got! So don't let him take the credit."

"But if it hadn't been for him . . ."

His father wouldn't let him finish. "Yeh, that's all I've heard this past year," he broke in impatiently. "Frank says this and Frank says that. Well, I'm sick of it. I'm not having another bloke playing father to my lad." He poked Frank in the chest with a stubby finger. "So from now on—leave him to me, OK?" And he walked away.

Barry's mother looked deeply embarrassed. "I'm sorry, Frank," she said softly, "really sorry . . ." She took Barry's arm. "Come on, love . . ."

Barry allowed himself to be led away, but as he reached the corner of the court, he glanced back. Frank was still standing in the same spot, looking after him with a hurt expression that Barry knew he would remember for the rest of his life.

They travelled back home by tube, his father prattling away about how lucky it was that he was out of work and could therefore devote all his time to Barry, about how wrong he had been to dismiss tennis as a career, and about how Frank had served his purpose but now he had to step aside.

Barry remained tight-lipped and silent. He couldn't forgive his father for the way he had given Frank the elbow, and the prospect of being coached by someone who didn't know anything about tennis appalled him. Suddenly the future, which an hour ago had seemed so rosy, was bleak and forbidding.

His father mistook his silence for ingratitude. He became surly and resentful, and that evening, as Barry was toying with his food, the volcano suddenly erupted.

"Come on, love," said his mother gently, "eat up."

"I'm not hungry."

"Feeling all right, are you?"

"Bit knackered. I'd like to go and lie down ..."

Barry rose from his chair, but his father pointed his fork at him. "You stay where you are, Barry. I'm not having any moodies from you, so you can just cut it out."

Barry resumed his seat, and his mother patted his arm. "He's tired, that's all. Aren't you, love?"

"Leave off," said his father contemptuously, "it's just his way of getting back at me." He munched his way through a mouthful of chips, then his tone softened. "Listen, son—I gave Frank his cards for a very good reason."

"What's that?" asked Barry.

"You was starting to lean on him too heavy. You got to learn to stand on your own two feet."

"I got a lot more than that to learn."

"I told you—I can teach you. I got nothing else to do, so I might as well make meself useful."

Barry looked down at his plate. "I need a proper coach. Every player needs one."

"I don't want to hear another word on the subject. You and me—we're going to make a great partnership."

It was incredible, thought Barry. The old man really thought he could take Frank's place. Well, he'd soon find out he couldn't. The trouble was he'd never admit it, and he'd certainly never let Barry go crawling back to Frank. There were definitely storm clouds ahead.

*

Two miles away, Lucy was also toying with her food. She felt utterly miserable—not because she'd lost, which was the reason her mother and father assumed she was in such a black mood, but because she now knew that she had been knocking herself out for nothing. They didn't really care if she won or lost. Nobody cared! So why should she care? The seven years that she had spent battling away in junior tournaments had been a complete waste of time.

She listened with mounting irritation as Wendy chattered away about the forthcoming drama school production in which she was to play Juliet. ". . . And the balcony scene!" she gushed. "You should see the set, Daddy. They've built this huge great wall—with a rose trellis so Romeo can come swarming up to me . . ."

"Hmm. Sounds exciting."

"And so romantic! It's all played by moonlight, you see. Mad passion under an Italian moon."

Lucy knew what her mother's reaction would be to that. Mad passion, like short skirts, wasn't her cup of tea at all. "Not too mad, I hope?" she asked predictably.

"But that's what it's all about, mother—burning, uncontrollable desire. If there's no mad passion, you might just as well not do the play . . ." Wendy flashed Lucy a sly glance. "You might just as well stage a tennis match or something."

Lucy couldn't think of a suitable reply before her father intervened. "They must think you're pretty good. To give you the leading part."

"Well at least it'll get me noticed," said Wendy smugly, "I've written to all the agents, and three of them have promised to come. So I'll be a bundle of nerves—which is why you've all simply got to be there."

"Wouldn't miss if for anything." Lucy, her head bent over her plate, felt her father turn towards her. "We'll all rally round, won't we, Lucy?"

"Oh yes," Lucy was dismayed to hear her voice trembling with anger, "we'll all rally round."

Her mother put down her knife and fork. "Something the matter, dear?"

"No."

Her father smiled. "Still haven't forgiven me, eh? Is that it?"

"Wendy never rallies round *me*," said Lucy sulkily. "So why should I rally round her?"

"Oh really." Wendy was doing her superior big-sister bit. "That's so childish . . ."

"Why? Tennis is as important to me as acting is for you. But you never come to see me play."

"This is different. I'm talking about my career . . ."

Lucy flared. "And I'm talking about mine! You all seem to think I'm going to give it up in a year or two and get a job as a secretary or something. Well, I'm not. I'm going to be a tennis player—and it's about time you stopped patting me on the head like a little dog and started taking me seriously."

There was an astonished silence. Then her father wiped his mouth with his napkin. "That's a little ungrateful, isn't it? We gave up our holiday to come and watch you."

"You didn't *watch* me, Daddy. You read your paper for a bit—then went off to the bar for half an hour. Wendy didn't come at all. And all Mummy's worried about is whether my skirt's too short."

"That's not true, darling," said her mother calmly, "I just want you to look nice, that's all."

"What does it matter? The only thing that matters is the result."

Wendy sighed theatrically. "Seems to me it matters too much, Beetle. You can't take defeat, that's your trouble. You're always in a grotty mood when you've lost."

This was too much. Lucy jumped to her feet, all the frustrations of the day boiling over. "And you know *why* I lost? Because my tennis doesn't mean anything to any of you—that's why. So I try to make it mean something by being successful—and end up by getting the elbow . . ." She paused and looked round the table. "Maybe I shouldn't care what you think—but I do. I can't help it. I just wish you cared as much what *I* thought."

And she ran out of the room.

*

Frank poured Judy another glass of wine. "You know what he said? He said 'I'm not having another bloke playing father to my lad.' That's what hurts."

"He must be very insecure."

"Insecure?"

"To feel so threatened."

"You think that's the reason?"

"Of course. He sounds like a very frightened man."

Frank stared at his wife. She was right, as usual. But it still didn't solve the problem. "I don't care about him," he said, running the tip of his forefinger round the rim of his wine-glass, "I care about Barry. If Grieves starts messing around with his game, it could ruin him."

Judy smiled. "If only kids could be born without parents . . ."

"It was asking for trouble, I suppose. Once I start offering a kid general guidance, I'm stepping into the parents' territory."

"At least now his father realises it *is* his territory."

"But now he's stepping into mine. And there's nothing I can do about it."

Judy put a sympathetic hand on his. "It's so unfair. After all your hard work . . ."

"Unfair on Barry too," said Frank gloomily. "He should take time out now—a couple of his strokes need taking apart and putting together again. But Grieves won't see that. He'll make the kid play in tournament after tournament—and his game'll gradually disintegrate . . ."

ELEVEN

"What'd you do that for?"

Barry glanced irritably over to the side of the court, where his father was peering through the netting like a middle-aged monkey. "Do what for?"

"Belted it away like that. No need to smack the cover off it."

"I didn't belt it. I just gave it too much topspin."

His father frowned, out of his depth. "Well, just forget about the fancy stuff. Get used to playing the percentages. Then it'll come natural during a match."

Lucy, who had been patiently bouncing a ball on the other side of the net, looked up and caught Barry's eye. He knew what she was thinking; if only the old man would get off his back. Off both their backs, because she had to put up with him too. He wondered how long it would be before she blew her top.

Since the Easter Tournament, they never got the chance to practise alone. The old man was always there, fingers curled round the netting, shouting at Barry whenever he hit the ball out and praising him when he was steady and unadventurous. "Play the percentages," he kept saying, and Barry could feel his confidence gradually ebbing away. He daren't experiment, try anything new or risky, for fear of incurring his father's wrath. Yet that's what practice-sessions were for; the thirty- or forty-stroke rallies that he and Lucy were encouraged to play all afternoon were garden party stuff. They were no preparation for the power-game of someone like Ken Maddox.

They started another rally, which ended when Barry, going for a winner down the line, hit another ball out.

His father shouted through the netting. "There you go—over-hitting again. Just keep the ball in the court, and let the other feller make the mistakes."

Barry felt like telling him to stuff it, but he took a deep breath and controlled himself. It was ridiculous—Borg and McEnroe didn't become Champs by playing the percentages. They took risks, went for the lines—which was what made them such exciting players.

He didn't want to hurt his father by telling him they'd get on much better without him. Nor did he want to provoke a row. But he decided to show him just how stupid his advice was.

So he began to take all the pace off the ball, sending it looping back high over the net. Lucy got the message immediately, and also started playing patball. The rally went on and on—fifty shots . . . sixty . . . seventy . . . eighty. Barry and Lucy started giggling; then the competitive instinct took over, and they gradually reduced the height and increased the pace of their shots until they were pounding the ball backwards and forwards with their old relish, both reluctant to make the error which would break such a long sequence.

Finally Barry, hitting deep to Lucy's backhand, approached the net. Lucy played cross-court to his own backhand, and he had a chance to play an easy volley down the line. But at the last moment, seeing that Lucy had it covered, he changed his mind and went for the more difficult cross-court volley, hoping to wrong-foot her. The angle was just too fine, however—and the ball went into the net.

His father's voice rang harshly across the court. "No excuse for missing that. You had a nice easy shot down the forehand."

"But she'd 've got it back," protested Barry.

"So what? You wouldn't 've lost the point, would you? You got to hang on and wait for the right opening."

This was too much. Barry opened his mouth, about to release all his pent-up frustration—but Lucy quickly intervened.

"I'm sorry, Mr Grieves," she called, looking at her watch, "I have to go now."

"OK. Same time tomorrow?"

Lucy glanced at Barry, who shrugged. "Right."

"Reckon I'll stop off for a quick one at the Crown and Anchor. See you back home, Barry."

Barry watched his father stride jauntily away, seemingly unaware of the havoc he was causing. But Lucy had obviously decided that the time had come for her to make her own protest.

She threw her racquet in her bag, and flopped down on a bench. "He's messing you up. You know that, don't you?"

Barry scuffed his feet on the shale. "Yeh."

"You've got to do something. And quick."

"What *can* I do?"

"Ask Frank to go on coaching you."

He stared at her. "Behind Dad's back?"

"If necessary."

"He'd kill me."

"He's killing you anyway. As a player."

This was true. But to go back to Frank would be to damage his old man's pride beyond repair. And the consequences could be very unpleasant. "He might kick me out. Get 'em to take me into care or something."

"Well, it's your decision. But a few more weeks of this, and even Frank won't be able to pick up the pieces."

Barry had often wondered whether he dared risk asking Frank to come back into his life, but decided it would cause too much bother with his father, who would never forgive him. On the way home, however, he began to give the idea serious thought. He knew now there was no way he could make it on his own, even if he didn't have his father breathing down his neck all the time. He needed professional help—so the question was, how much was he willing to sacrifice for it?

He was sure his mother would understand. She at least realised how important Frank's coaching was and had pleaded with his father to change his mind. Yes, she'd understand—but she probably wouldn't approve. An easy-going woman who liked a quiet life, she'd never encourage Barry to go against his father's wishes.

But if he *didn't* go against them, what was there left to look forward to? A few more tournaments, a gradual decline in his game—then perhaps that office job if he was lucky! And there were bound to be rows with his father anyway; Barry was finding it more and more difficult to control his temper when he was shouting all that ignorant rubbish from the side of the court. Whatever he decided, an explosion seemed imminent—so what had he got to lose? He changed direction towards Frank's flat.

It was Judy, Frank's wife, who opened the door. Barry had met her several times before when Frank had invited him back to tea after a lesson, but he had never really got to know her. He knew she was a teacher, and all teachers made him nervous, though he'd never seen such a pretty one before. And he'd begun to realise that she did a lot of Frank's thinking for him. She didn't speak much, but when she did Frank gave her all of his attention. She was definitely the power behind the throne.

She seemed genuinely pleased to see him, and she and Frank listened carefully as he made his pitch. Disappointingly, however, Frank shook his head. "I can't go on teaching you, Barry—I just can't. Your father's warned me off."

"Well supposing you didn't take no notice? What could he do?"

"He could get a court order forbidding me to speak to you. Imagine how that'd look in the papers."

"But I'll never make it on me own."

"Then find another coach. There are plenty of good ones around. I'll give you a list . . ."

"Forget it," said Barry gloomily. "If Dad's given *you* the push, he's not going to let no one else take over, is he?"

Frank shrugged helplessly, "I wish I could help—but I can't. You see that, don't you?"

"I'll run away. That's what I'll do. Just—take off."

"How would you live?"

"What about Mr Bousfield?"

"He promised to sponsor you, not support you. And he wouldn't want to get involved with runaways."

Barry, realising that there was nothing left to say, stood up and moved to the door. He was sure the battle was lost, but reinforcements arrived from an unexpected quarter.

"Why don't you sleep on it, Frank?" asked Judy quietly. "Give him your decision tomorrow?"

Barry turned, to see Frank looking puzzled. "I've just given him my answer."

"I think we ought to talk about it."

Frank stared at her, then nodded.

"Thanks, Mrs Abbott," said Barry gratefully.

She moved to the door and opened it for him. "Keep your fingers crossed, Barry," she whispered, "no game's lost till the final whistle."

He went out, but hovered outside the flat, listening. He felt guilty eavesdropping on their conversation, but he just had to know what his chances were.

"What was all that about?" he heard Frank saying. "You think I'm wrong?"

Judy's voice was clearer. She was obviously still standing by the door. "I just think you should take more time before making up your mind."

"It's already made up, Judy. I couldn't take the responsibility."

"What about your responsibility to Barry? He didn't ask you to come into his life—that was your decision."

A pause. Then a barely audible "I know" from Frank.

Judy's voice grew fainter as she moved away from the door. "He needs you, Frank. You're the one who gave him hope—who opened the gate to the magic garden and showed him all the goodies that lay within his reach. So you can't just stand by and let his father shut it again, can you?"

Barry had heard enough. He knew that however long it took, Judy was going to persuade Frank to start teaching him again. He turned and ran down the stairs two at a time.

*

He didn't have to wait long. Next day, as he came out of school, he saw Frank's car parked on the opposite side of the street.

He dashed over the zebra crossing and climbed in beside him "You decided then?" he asked eagerly.

"*I've* decided," said Frank. "But have you?"

"Eh?"

"Have you really thought this through, Barry? What's your father going to say?"

"He's going to go spare."

"Exactly. And is it worth all the flak?" Barry nodded.

Frank stared at him searchingly for a long moment, then

turned and started the engine. "All right. You're the one that has to live with him." He signalled, and edged the car into the stream of afternoon traffic.

"Where are we going?" asked Barry.

"Private court. Belongs to a friend of Mr Bousfield's. He's away for three months, so we won't be disturbed."

"What about Lucy? She'll be waiting for me at the Club."

Frank smiled. "I phoned her and told her you wouldn't be coming. It's your father you'll have to make your peace with."

"Yeh." It wouldn't be pleasant, thought Barry, but he was prepared to pay the price. Anyway, he didn't have to face him for another couple of hours. He was back with Frank, that was the main thing.

They drove to a quiet, shady street lined by some of the largest houses Barry had ever seen. Each stood in its own garden, surrounded by trees; each had its own driveway, and several had large, shiny cars standing outside the front doors.

Frank turned in through the iron gate of a house called "Ferndown", and parked by the garage. Barry got out and stared in awe at the shuttered windows. "Blimey, what a gaff! Got any kids, has he? This geezer?"

"No idea," said Frank. "Why?"

"Maybe he'll adopt me."

Frank grabbed him by the arm and spun him round. "You've got a father, Barry—a father who's proud of you. That's worth far more than a house like this."

Barry wondered why on earth Frank thought his father was proud of him; all he'd ever done was put obstacles in his way. But he didn't argue. If Frank wanted to believe that, it was probably because he felt guilty.

They walked round to the back of the house, and followed a narrow path through the bushes to a hard court and a swimming pool at the end of the garden. Though it was now late spring, both were covered with leaves and twigs—the debris of the winter winds—and before they could play, they had to clear the court.

"You reckon *I'll* make enough to buy a place like this?" asked Barry, sweeping a pile of leaves into a corner.

Frank was measuring the net with two of his steel racquets. "Not unless we do something about your backhand."

Barry grinned. "Nothing wrong with *your* backhand. And *you* don't live here."

"That's because I give too many free lessons. Come on—let's get to work."

It was like old times, thought Barry, as he happily swallowed Frank's scathing comments about his game. How could he have forgotten all his technique in the few weeks since the Easter Tournament? Had it all gone in one ear and out the other? Why was he playing like an old woman, frightened to go for his shots? Where was his footwork, his follow-through, his power? If he wanted to play patball, why didn't he find three other women and make up a doubles? And so on.

Barry lapped it up. He stopped playing safe and started taking risks, his confidence flowing back. He had never known a lesson pass so quickly, and he could hardly believe it when Frank told him the hour was up. He had completely forgotten about his father, but now the prospect of an imminent confrontation hung over him like a cloud. How on earth was he going to break the news?

*

Though Barry didn't know it, the news had already been broken. When he didn't turn up at the Club, his father walked round to the school to find out if he'd been kept late for some reason. He met Mr Miller in the playground, who happened to have seen Barry get into a car and drive off.

From the description, there was no doubt that the car belonged to Frank.

In a towering rage, Mr Grieves walked straight round to Frank's flat. On the way, he rehearsed his speech; if he didn't get a full apology and a promise never to see Barry again, he'd go to the law.

He was disconcerted when Frank's wife answered the door. She was very pretty—far prettier than Barry's description—and for a moment he was at a loss for words. He couldn't use the ones he'd thought of using in front of a lady.

He was still seething with anger, however, and he made no attempt to hide it. "Where is he?" he growled menacingly.

"If you mean my husband," she said coolly, "he's teaching."

"I said where?"

She stared at him. "You're Barry's father?"

He nodded. She stood aside to allow him to enter. "You'd better come in."

He walked past her into the room, then turned to face her. "Frank's giving Barry a lesson, right? Behind my back?"

"Yes."

"Bleeding nerve."

"How did you find out?"

"Never mind. I want to know where they are."

She indicated a chair. "Please—sit down." Reluctantly, he sat opposite her. "I don't know where they are, Mr Grieves—really. Frank said something about a private court . . ."

"Wait till I get hold of 'em. I've a good mind to give 'em both a thumping."

"You might as well thump me too."

"You?"

"Frank didn't want to go against your wishes. I persuaded him to change his mind."

He frowned, puzzled. "Why?"

"Because Barry needs him."

"He needs Barry, you mean. Just can't let go, can he?"

She smiled, taking the sting out of her words. "Seems to me *you're* the one who can't let go, Mr Grieves."

"Listen," he said indignantly, "he's my kid. If Frank wants to play God, he should've had kids of his own . . ." Then, realising he'd gone too far: "Sorry. Out of order, that. Sorry."

She lit a cigarette, and blew a cloud of smoke into the air. "You mean, Frank has no rights at all? After giving up hours of his time?"

"Nobody twisted his arm, Mrs Abbott. And we didn't make him no promises."

"So you don't feel you owe him anything?"

"I'm not saying we're not grateful. But now we don't need him no more. So he's just got to do as he's told and step out of the picture."

She gazed at him with calm blue eyes. "What are you afraid of, Mr Grieves?"

"Eh?"

"You're frightened of Frank, aren't you? Because you think Barry's beginning to respect him more than you. But you're never going to make him respect you by letting him see how jealous you are."

He jumped to his feet, his anger welling up again. He wasn't going to sit here and be lectured like a little kid. "I don't have to take that from you," he said grimly.

"No, you don't. You can leave whenever you like."

He marched to the door and wrenched it open. "You can give your husband a message from me. I've warned him once, and I'm not going to warn him again. If he won't leave Barry alone, I'll go to the law." And he stormed out of the flat, banging the door behind him.

So when Barry arrived home, no explanations were necessary. He found his father pacing round the living-room and his mother sitting in a chair, placidly sewing. Both of them knew where he'd been.

"Well?" his father demanded as soon as he appeared in the doorway. "What've you got say for yourself?"

"About what?" asked Barry, playing for time.

"You know bleeding well about what! I been to see Mrs Abbott."

"Oh."

"That all you got to say? After sneaking round to Frank behind me back?"

Barry shrugged. "I was going to tell you. It was the first time."

"And the last. I warned his wife—any more under-the-counter lessons, and I'll have the law on him."

"No need to get heavy."

"Should've kept away from you then, shouldn't he?"

"I was the one that didn't keep away."

His father stared at him in disgust. "That's gratitude, that is. After I've given up every afternoon to coach you . . ."

"But you *can't* coach me, Dad," said Barry gently. "You don't know nothing about tennis."

"Well you can take your choice. It's me or nobody."

"OK. I'll pack it in."

"You can't. I've entered you for three tournaments next month."

Barry shook his head firmly. "Frank says I've got to take time out. No more tournaments till he's put me game right."

"You don't need him. I can do that."

"No, Dad. If you won't let me have proper coaching, I'm not playing in no more tournaments. It'd be like fighting with one hand tied behind me back."

"You'll do what I tell you . . ."

Barry's mother spoke for the first time. "You can't make him play if he doesn't want to, Jack."

"Now don't you start ..."

She put down her sewing. "It's about time I had my say. You're just being selfish."

"Selfish? That's nice, that is. I give up all me spare time ..."

She stared at him, her head on one side like a bird. "For Barry's sake? Or yours?"

"Eh?"

"You can't bear the thought of someone else taking the credit, can you? You never lifted a finger to help Barry till Frank came on the scene. And now you're all over him—and making a fool of yourself into the bargain."

"Who says?"

"I say. Barry's right—you don't know the first thing about tennis. And as for threatening poor Frank with the law— anybody'd think he was trying to do the boy some harm ..."

Jack Grieves blinked as if she had struck him. "I'm just trying to be a good father, that's all."

"Good fathers want the best for their kids. They don't stand in their way."

"I'm not standing in his way—I'm trying to help him. If he don't want to know, that's down to him."

"Just like it's down to me whether I cook your supper or not."

"What are you on about?"

"If you want to be pig-headed, you can fetch your own food. Barry and me'll eat on our own."

Barry could hardly believe his ears, it was the first time he'd ever heard his mother talk back to his father, and he watched with amazement as she calmly put her sewing back in her bag and went out.

Barry's father stared after her, open-mouthed, then followed her. He stood just outside the door, shouting towards the kitchen. "All right—he can go on with his bleeding lessons. But that's the finish. I don't want nothing more to do with him." And he disappeared up the stairs.

Barry remained rooted to the spot. So that was that. He had told himself he was prepared to pay the price, but now he wasn't so sure. His tennis-life might be sorted out, but his home-life looked like being a real pain.

*

Lucy's parents had gone to bed. Wendy, however, flushed from her success as Juliet, had asked Lucy to stay up and keep her company for a while, so they sat at opposite ends of the kitchen table, sipping glasses of hot milk.

"Well?" said Wendy.

Lucy hadn't yet told her what she thought of her performance, as relations between them were still strained from the row they'd had after the Easter Tournament. But she'd been genuinely impressed; there was no doubt that her sister had talent as an actress, and it was evident the audience thought so too. They had given her a tremendous ovation when she took her curtain call, and Lucy had felt proud of her. She had no intention of telling her, however—she was far too big-headed already.

"Well what?" she asked innocently.

"What did you think?"

Lucy toyed with her glass. "I thought you were OK."

"Just OK?"

Wendy, still in her stage make-up, was regarding her anxiously. Lucy was pleasantly surprised; her sister really seemed to want her opinion. "The audience liked you," she said, "what's it matter what *I* think?"

"Of course it matters. You can never trust what agents and

people tell you. But you can trust what your own family tells you."

"Well Mummy and Daddy liked you too."

"They're just doting parents. I want to know how my non-doting sister liked me?"

Lucy smiled. "I thought you were great."

"Really?"

"Really."

Wendy smiled back. "In that case, maybe I'll come to your next tournament."

"No need to go mad."

"It's only fair. You supported me—I should support you."

"You'd be bored stiff."

"No, I wouldn't. As a matter of fact . . ." Wendy hesitated, looking embarrassed.

"What?"

"I rather enjoy tennis. Watching it, I mean."

Lucy searched her face for a sign that she was taking the mickey, but she seemed perfectly serious. "So why didn't you come before?"

"I was jealous, I suppose."

"Jealous?"

Wendy cupped her hands around the glass, feeling the warmth of the milk. "I always wanted to be good at games," she said awkwardly. "But at school—on the hockey field and the netball court—I was a joke. The other girls used to groan whenever I was put in the same team. So I pretended it was all a big drag."

It was an extraordinary admission. Lucy had never dreamed that her beautiful sister could possibly be jealous; she had so much going for her. But now she'd revealed her secret, she suddenly seemed vulnerable.

"Well you can't have everything," said Lucy softly.

"I know. But whatever you don't have—it's always the thing you want."

They sipped their milk in silence for a moment. Then Lucy grinned. "Tell you what. I'll swap my forehand for your figure."

"Done."

They shook hands across the table to cement the deal.

TWELVE

Once more it was summer. Barry had a private court for his lessons, a Club for his practice-sessions with Lucy and a sponsor to take care of his expenses. His troubles should have been over—but there was still the problem of his father, whose brooding, implacable presence hung over the warm, sunny days like a pall.

The rift was now complete. His mother did her best to bring them together, to include his father in the conversation, and Barry himself made repeated attempts to break through his father's wall of hostility. But all they received in return were a few surly grunts and an occasional sarcastic remark aimed at the air above their heads.

The atmosphere at home was so depressing that it became difficult to concentrate on tennis. Barry could see the effect it was having on his mother, how sometimes her eyes filled with tears when she failed to coax his father out of his shell—and he couldn't help feeling guilty. He didn't want her to suffer, but it seemed that she had not been forgiven for taking his side.

He followed the results of the Junior tournaments in the papers, and Lucy, whose own form seemed to be getting progressively worse, filled in the details. She herself had reached two Finals early on in the summer, but in the next three competitions was knocked out in the first or second rounds. In the boys' events, Chetwyn, it seemed, was the rising star. In the absence of Ken Maddox, whose eighteenth birthday had fallen just after the Easter Tournament and who was consequently no longer eligible, his old rival was cleaning up. There was an article about him in one of the posh newspapers which Barry read in Mr Ferris's shop under the heading *Britain's New Hope?*, and he couldn't help feeling a pang of jealousy.

He was pleased with his own progress, however—and he knew that Frank was pleased too. The kinks in his backhand and service action had been ironed out, and he was confident that both strokes would now stand up to the pressure of match-play. He waited eagerly for Frank to tell him he was ready for the tournament circuit again, but he didn't press it. He trusted Frank's judgement, and it was for him to decide when that moment had arrived.

One evening, towards the end of July, he was sitting in the kitchen with his mother and father, munching his way through a plate of egg and chips and trying to ignore the oppressive silence that had descended over the table. It was always worst at meal-times because there was no escape. And his father was making it even more difficult than usual to get through to him; hunched over his summer pools coupon, he was trying to decide which eight Australian football matches were most likely to end in score-draws.

Barry caught his mother's eye, which stirred her into making one of her sporadic efforts at conversation. "What did you do today, love?" she asked, sounding unnaturally cheerful.

"Worked on me service. I've got real sidespin on it now."

"Sidespin? That's way above my head." She turned to her husband. "What's sidespin, Jack?"

"Ask *him*," he said, without looking up, "he's the expert."

Barry saw his mother blink back tears, and came quickly

to her rescue. "You hit across the ball like this, Mum." He demonstrated his service action. "Gives you more control."

The doorbell rang. He jumped up eagerly, relieved at the excuse to leave the table, and rushed to answer it.

Frank was standing on the doorstep. "Hi," he said, smiling.

"Hi." Barry opened the door wider. "Come in."

"You'd better ask your Dad first. He may not want me to darken his threshold."

"Don't be funny . . ."

"No, Barry. Go on—ask him."

So Barry went back to the kitchen. "It's Frank. Can he come in?"

His father was still filling in his coupon. "No," he growled, "tell him to shove off."

"It could be important."

"Not to me. If he wants to talk to you, he can do it outside."

Barry's mother put down her knife and fork. "Oh Jack! Don't be such an old bear . . ."

"I'm not having him in my house. And that's final!"

Barry returned to the front door and shrugged apologetically. "Sorry, Frank . . ."

"It's OK. I understand."

"More than I do."

"Wait till you have kids of your own."

"So what's this all about then?"

Frank leaned against the doorpost. "I've had a call from Peter Hastings. Asking how you were coming along."

"Peter Hastings? Thought he'd crossed me off his list since Bisham."

"He can't afford to. He hasn't got that amount of talent at his disposal."

"What did you tell him?"

"That you were coming along fine. And that you were ready."

"What for?"

"The big one."

Barry frowned. "Big one?"

"There's a new National Junior Invitation Tournament down in Eastbourne. The climax of the whole year. And Peter's inviting you."

"When is it?"

"End of August. The winner will join the Davis Cup team for Senior Squad Training."

"Davis Cup team? Blimey."

It was clear from Frank's expression that as far as he was concerned, this *was* the big one. "We've got a month, Barry," he said quietly. "You'd better start stepping up your roadwork."

Barry had always considered himself to be pretty fit, but when he started to add an evening run to his morning paper round he realised he still had some way to go before he reached his peak. By pushing himself harder and harder, he discovered hidden reserves of energy, previously untapped. Lucy appointed herself as his trainer, accompanying him on her bike and urging him on whenever he looked like flagging.

Usually, her scathing remarks about his lack of stamina and guts made him keep going. But one evening, running up the hill towards Alexandra Palace, he suddenly knew he couldn't make it to the top. Lungs bursting and legs wobbling, he collapsed on to the grass verge beside the road.

Lucy dismounted and wheeled her bike over to him. "What's the problem?"

He lay on his back with his eyes closed, gasping for air. "You're joking."

"On your feet, Champ. Only another three miles to go."

"Forget it." He opened his eyes and rolled over on his side, resting his head on his elbow. "Dunno what I'm killing meself for anyway."

She frowned down at him. "Frank's orders. If you don't complete the course, he might sack me as your trainer."

"I'm serious," said Barry gloomily, "maybe the whole thing isn't worth it."

"Course it is! Think of Eastbourne. You don't want to run out of puff, do you?"

"I didn't mean the training. I meant . . ."

"Meant what?"

"Me old man. It's terrible at home. He don't hardly speak to me."

"Because of Frank?" He nodded. "But that's childish."

"I know. It's getting me down, though. Me mum too. She tries not to let on, but it's tearing her apart."

Lucy looked thoughtful. "Tell you what. Why don't you come back to tea?"

This was the first time she had invited him back to her house. She had never introduced him to her mother, though he had seen her in the distance at both the the County Under-sixteens and the Easter Tournament, and he had always assumed that she was ashamed of him. He didn't blame her, because her family were posh, and he was just a yobbo. But one day, as they were leaving the Club, she had unexpectedly apologised for not returning his mother's hospitality, confiding that it was her own family she was ashamed of. They were so dreary, she said, and she was sure he'd be bored to tears with them.

For some reason, however, she had changed her mind. Perhaps she just felt sorry for him. But whatever had prompted the invitation, he glady accepted it; at least he wouldn't have to face his father again for another hour or so.

The Roberts' house was not on his paper round, but he knew the street well because three of Mr Ferris's customers lived in it—two *Guardians* and a *Times*. It was on the top of the hill at the north end of his patch—the high point of his round where the air always tasted cooler and sweeter.

Lucy led him through the back door to the kitchen, where she poured him a glass of milk and piled sandwiches on to a plate. Then she took him into the living-room to introduce him to her parents.

To his surprise, they made him feel welcome. They listened with interest as Lucy explained about the problem with his father, and seemed genuinely sympathetic. He couldn't understand why Lucy thought them dreary; he couldn't imagine either of them not speaking to her for weeks because she'd done something they didn't approve of.

"You mustn't give up, Barry," said Mr Roberts, after he had heard the whole story. "Seems to me the best way of proving your father wrong is to go ahead and win this tournament."

"I don't want to prove him wrong," Barry told him miserably, "I just want him in my corner."

"Sounds like hurt pride, that's all. He'll get over it."

"Won't come down to Eastbourne, though. Says he can't afford it."

"What about your mother?" asked Mrs Roberts.

"Oh, *she's* coming. Frank's driving her down, and she's staying with me Aunt Winnie in Brighton. But Dad—he'd never accept nothing from Frank. Not even a lift."

"Maybe he'll change his mind. There's still a week to go."

Barry shook his head. "No. Thing is—I told him I didn't need him. I meant as a coach, but he took it the wrong way."

Mr Roberts collected his wife's glass and moved to the sideboard to refill it. "And now he thinks you don't need him at all?"

"Right."

"Couldn't you explain it was all a misunderstanding?"

"I've tried. But he just walks out on me."

"Well at least you'll have *some* support. Your mother . . . Frank . . ."

"And me," put in Lucy. "Can I go, Daddy? Frank says I can stay with him and Mrs Abbott."

Mr Roberts glanced at his wife. "I don't see why not. If Barry lost because he didn't have his trainer with him, we'd never hear the end of it."

"Great." She stuffed a sandwich in her mouth and stood up. "Come on, Champ. You can do your last three miles on the running track."

Barry groaned. "Real hard case, this bird of yours." He followed her to the door. "Thanks for the tea."

Mrs Roberts smiled. "You're welcome, Barry. Sorry we didn't have any cake."

"Forget it, Mother," said Lucy scornfully. "His mum makes much better cakes than you do."

"I wouldn't take that from her, Mrs Roberts." Barry was amazed at the ease with which he could talk to Lucy's parents. "If she belonged to me, I'd put her on bread and butter for a week."

They went out, leaving Mr and Mrs Roberts sipping their drinks thoughtfully. "Poor kid," said Mr Roberts quietly.

"Yes," said Mrs Roberts. "That father of his—I just don't understand how he could be so selfish."

"Don't you?"

She stared at him in surprise. "Why are you looking at me like that?"

"We've been just as bad, you know. Maybe worse."

"George, what *are* you talking about?"

"I'm talking about Lucy. She needs us just as much as Barry needs his father. And we've let her down."

"Let her down? How?"

Mr Roberts gulped down the rest of his drink. "We've

never treated her tennis seriously. Never given her the same sort of support and encouragement we give to Wendy."

"I don't know what you mean. I go to all her tournaments . . ."

"It's not just being there. It's taking an interest. Appreciating her success."

Mrs Roberts frowned. "What brought all this on? That little outburst after the Easter Tournament?"

"Yes. It's been worrying me ever since. Because she was right—it's never really mattered to us whether she won or lost, has it?"

"Not to you, perhaps . . ."

"To either of us. But it matters to Lucy—more than anything in the world."

Mrs Roberts considered this in silence for a moment. "I thought this tennis thing was just a passing phase . . ."

"Maybe it is—but at least we ought to give it a chance. If she's got this far *without* our support, think how far she could go *with* it."

*

Devonshire Park lies just behind the seafront in Eastbourne. Its complex of superb grass courts belongs to the Corporation, at the service of the community whenever it is not being used for tournaments. In the week before Wimbledon, it is the venue for an important Grand Prix event in which most of the world's top women players take part, and in August the National Junior Grass Court Championships also take place there.

The Invitation Tournament was a new competition, an exclusive event for the best young players of the year; a last chance for some to improve their rankings, for others to establish their supremacy.

In the Boys Under-sixteen section, it soon became clear

that there were only two possible winners—Chetwyn, seeded number one, and Barry, seeded number two. Both were way ahead of the rest of the field, brushing their early-round opponents aside with no difficulty. They were like two gun-fighters, clearing the decks for the final showdown.

All through the week, they eyed each other warily, watching each others' matches in the hope of spotting weaknesses they could exploit. Barry couldn't help being impressed with Chetwyn; his progress over the past year had been spectacular, and there was now no need for him to use gamesmanship. The article in *The Times* was no exaggeration; he looked an extremely exciting prospect.

But Barry knew that he, too, had improved—how much, only time would tell. His absence from the circuit had given Chetwyn a clear run through the summer, and he had the disadvantage of not having played a tournament since Easter, but with every match, as he grew used to the faster pace of the grass courts, his confidence grew. And he could see that Chetwyn was worried; several times during the week he had caught sight of his rival watching him with a thoughtful frown.

Saturday arrived—the day of the showdown. The finals were to be played on the centre court, surrounded on three sides by spectators' enclosures. And they were being televised by the BBC as part of "Summer Grandstand". Barry felt the old sinking feeling in the pit of his stomach; he'd never played in front of a hundred people before, let alone millions.

His mother had phoned his father with the news that he had reached the Final, and he wondered if the old man would now let bygones be bygones and come down for the match. He jumped eagerly off the Brighton bus and rushed round the courts—but there was no sign of him, and he returned dejectedly to the pavilion.

Lucy, dressed in a track-suit, was waiting with his mother. "He's not here, Barry," she said sadly, "I looked, too."

His mother put a sympathetic hand on his arm. "He's a proud man, love. Proud and stubborn. Just like you."

Barry grinned, hiding his disappointment. "Should've been a tennis player then, shouldn't he?" He looked round. "Where's Frank?"

"Talking to Peter Hastings," said Lucy. "He asked me to give you this." She leaned forwards and gave him a quick peck on the cheek.

He stared at her in astonishment. "I didn't know he cared."

"Well he does. We all do. You want to start knocking up?"

"Why, what's the time?"

"Half-past one. And you're on at two."

"OK." Barry turned to his mother. "Got your pass, Mum?"

"Don't you worry about me, son." She squeezed his hand. "Good luck."

She moved away, joining the crowd of spectators converging on the centre court. Barry and Lucy walked to one of the outside courts near the entrance to the park, and started knocking up.

Every day they had gone through the same ritual, with Lucy unselfishly acting as Barry's sparring partner. Barry felt sorry for her; she hadn't been invited to take part in the tournament, as she was now too old for the Under-sixteen division and her results weren't good enough for the Under-eighteens. But she didn't seem to mind; some day, she said, when he thanked her for her help, he would do the same for her.

He kept one eye on the entrance, hoping that his father might still appear. It was a faint hope, he knew, but there was still time. As the clock above the centre court moved slowly towards two, however, hope grew even fainter.

At five to two, Lucy glanced at her watch. "You'd better go."

Barry stood staring at the entrance, where the flood of spectators had dwindled to a trickle. "Hang on a minute. He might still come."

"You can't afford to hang on a minute. It's nearly time."

He waited a few more seconds, then reluctantly moved away. Outside the gate, Lucy raised her fist in a silent gesture of encouragement, and hurried away to take her seat in the stand. Barry showed his pass to the gate-keeper, who nodded and let him through.

Chetwyn was waiting impatiently by the umpire's chair. "Late again, old son," he said as Barry appeared. "Didn't work last time, did it? And it's not going to work this."

But Barry had no intention of losing his cool. He had prepared himself carefully for this match, and was determined not to get involved in a verbal battle. He held out his racquet. "Call it."

Chetwyn seemed in no hurry. "I promised you a real spanking, remember?" he said, smiling arrogantly. "Next time we met?"

"You going to call? Or go on rabbiting all day?"

"Rough."

Barry spun the racquet, then picked it up and held it out for Chetwyn's inspection. "You want to check?"

Chetwyn peered closely at the racquet and nodded. "Well?"

"I'll serve."

"I'll take that end."

As the players moved to opposite ends of the court, Peter Hastings, sitting in the stand next to Frank and Judy, watched them with intense interest. "Funny, isn't it? They should be meeting in the Final?"

"I don't think Barry finds it funny," said Frank softly.

"You reckon there's going to be another punch-up?"

"Depends how much he's taken in. Some of these kids—you think you've got through to 'em in practice, but the moment they're under pressure they forget it all."

"Well, you've certainly done wonders with this one," said Hastings, as Barry sent a series of practice-serves crashing into the left-hand court, "Getting him this far without a single blow-up."

Frank smiled. "I can't promise you a saint."

"I wouldn't want one. But I always knew he had talent. It really hurt, having to send him home from Bisham."

Judy raised a sceptical eyebrow. "Hurt you more than him, eh?"

"Had to be done, Judy," said Hastings firmly. "These Regional Training groups are supposed to work together, not beat the daylights out of each other. Let's hope he's learned his lesson."

Frank settled back in his seat. "Well, we'll soon know."

*

Far away in North London, Mr Grieves was opening a can of beer. He sat down tensely on the edge of his chair, staring at the television set. On the screen, the umpire was announcing the match to the crowd: "The Final of the National Junior Invitation Tournament—Boys Under-sixteen section. Grieves to serve. Play . . ."

THIRTEEN

"Game to Chetwyn. First game."

Barry tried not to let his disappointment show. He'd lost his first serve to love—two muffed volleys and two good returns from his opponent—which was a bad psychological blow.

Chetwyn grinned at him during the changeover. "Come on, old son. Make a match of it."

Barry ignored him, walking calmly across to the opposite end of the court.

Chetwyn's first serve was deep to the forehand. Barry flashed at it, and sent a low cross-court return skimming over the net, well out of Chetwyn's reach.

"Love–fifteen."

Another serve. Another winning cross-court return.

"Love–thirty."

The next serve was heavily sliced, down the centre line. There was little Barry could do about it, except make sure his return went into court. Chetwyn was in a position to make a winning volley, but netted it.

"Love–forty."

Chetwyn frowned, walked slowly back to the baseline and served again. Again the heavy slice, curving in to Barry's body. But Barry, gambling, had moved round to take it on his forehand and sent a crashing drive down the line.

"Game to Grieves. The games are one-all. First set."

Loud applause rang round the court. Barry breathed a sigh of relief; he was back in the match. Not only that, but by breaking his opponent's service to love he had given him something to think about. He felt much better.

His first serve of the third game was a sizzling ace down the centre line.

"Fifteen–love."

Barry moved across to the left-hand court, but to his surprise Chetwyn made no move to take up the receiving position. He was standing, hands on hips, staring indignantly at the umpire.

"You're joking."

"Fifteen–love," repeated the umpire tonelessly.

"That was a fault."

"The ball was in. Fifteen–love."

"Oh come on! It wasn't even close . . ."

"Play on, please."

Chetwyn turned to the spectators behind him. "You see that?" he demanded. "It was a mile out, right?"

The umpire looked at his watch. "You have thirty seconds, Chetwyn. If you don't play on, I shall award a penalty point against you."

Chetwyn glared at him. Then, realising that further protest was useless walked slowly across to the left-hand court. Barry, who had been patiently bouncing a ball on his racquet, served again—into the net.

Chetwyn held up his hand. "Hold it!" he called, and bent down to tie his shoelace.

Up in the stands, Lucy, sitting with Barry's mother, reacted angrily. 'Up to his old tricks again," she muttered.

Mrs Grieves blinked at her. "You mean he's doing that on purpose? To put Barry off?"

"Yes. He's well known for it."

"Someone should punch his head in."

Lucy laughed. "It's already been tried, remember?"

Down on the court, Chetwyn, having attended to his shoelace, indicated that he was now ready to resume. Barry grinned at him, to let him know that he knew what his opponent was up to—but that he didn't care.

"Second service," called the umpire.

Barry used his newly-acquired sidespin to make the ball kick, and sent over a perfectly placed serve deep to the backhand corner. Chetwyn completely mistimed his return, ballooning it way out of court.

"Thirty–love."

Judy nodded her approval. "Good boy."

"Yes," said Hastings thoughtfully, "Six months ago, there'd 've been steam coming out of his ears."

It proved to be the turning point of the match. Chetwyn, seeming to realise that whatever he did Barry was not going to be put off, didn't bother to try any more tricks. And having lost the first set on a tie-break, he put up only token resistance in the second. Barry won it easily, six–two.

At the end of the match, Chetwyn offered him a grudging hand. "You were lucky," he said sourly.

"No, old son," Barry said. "Last time—you was lucky."

"Why?"

" 'Cos we didn't have no umpire."

He collected his spare racquet and left the court, the applause of the crowd still ringing in his ears.

Peter Hastings was waiting for him, standing with Frank and his wife, Lucy and his mother. "Well done, Barry," he said, offering his hand. "Great match."

"Thanks, Mr Hastings."

"I shall need you back at Bisham next month. To start training with the Davis Cup team."

This was music to Barry's ears. "OK," he said happily.

"Hang on a minute." His mother pulled Hastings round to face her. "You're the one who sent him home last year?"

"That's right," said Hastings.

"How do we know you won't do it again?"

"You don't. But maybe you and your husband would like to come down to Bisham too? You can keep this young tearaway in order, and we can talk about his future."

She glanced at Frank. "He's the one you want to talk to."

"No," Hastings told her firmly. "Frank's done his job. Now it's up to you and me." He moved away to talk to the two girls who were just going on court.

Typical, thought Barry. Now he'd become a serious prospect, they wanted to give Frank the brush-off.

His mother was obviously thinking along the same lines. "You're not going to let that feller cut you out, are you Frank? Not going to let him take the credit after all your hard work?"

But Frank seemed to think it was quite natural. "I'm used to it, Mrs Grieves. And Peter's right—it's time Barry left school and went on to university. Don't worry—he'll be in good hands."

"But—what about you? Don't you get nothing out of it?"

"I told you when we first met—it's kids like Barry that make my job worthwhile. Every time he wins, he wins for both of us. And when he wins Wimbledon, I'll share his victory. Though he'll have forgotten all about me by then."

"Not while I'm around, he won't." Barry gasped as his mother's elbow dug into his ribs.

"He's not going to forget me either," announced Lucy loudly. "Because we're going to win the Mixed Doubles together."

Barry grinned at her. "Have to do something about your serve, then. It's pathetic."

Lucy's eyes widened with mock indignation. "Listen to him. Win's a tin-pot little tournament, and thinks he's Jimmy Connors."

The Tannoy suddenly blared from the pavilion. "Telephone call for Barry Grieves. Barry Grieves—wanted on the phone ..."

Barry stared at his mother. "I wonder if that's ..."

She smiled. "There's only one way to find out, love."

He turned and raced along the path to the pavilion. Inside, one of the tournament officials indicated a phone with the receiver off the hook. He picked it up, his throat dry. "Yeh?"

"Barry?" It was his father's voice. "It's me."

Barry's heart jumped, but he tried to sound casual. "Oh—hello, Dad. Did you watch it?"

"Course. And I just wanted to say—well done."

"Thanks. I'm sorry you wasn't here."

"I'm sorry too, Maybe next time, eh?"

"Yeh."

"Well—that's all, Barry. See you later."

"Right. And thanks for ringing, Dad." He replaced the receiver and stood staring at it for a long moment. What was it footballers kept saying? *Over the moon.* Yes, that just about summed it up.

His mother was still standing with Lucy, Frank and Judy outside the centre court. She raised her eyebrows anxiously as he ran up. "Was it ...?"

"Yeh."

She squeezed his arm, her eyes moistening. "Good."

"Well I'd better go and phone Mr Bousfield," said Frank. "Tell him his long shot has started to pay off."

"Maybe he'll give me a bonus," said Barry cheekily.

"He won't want to talk about bonuses. He'll want to talk about plastering his company logo all over your gear."

He walked away. Barry's mother watched him, shaking

her head in sympathy. "I feel so sorry for him. Now he's got to start all over again."

"Kids grow up, Mrs Grieves," said Judy, "they can't just stand still. All teachers have that problem."

"Parents too." Barry felt his mother slip her arm through his. "Come on, Champ. You don't have to move on for a few years yet. Let's go home."

And they walked slowly through the maze of sunlit courts towards the entrance.

This story is based on the BBC TV series *Break Point* first shown in 1982. It was produced by Paul Stone and directed by Roger Singleton-Turner. The main characters who appear in the book were played as follows: Barry, Ian Barker; Lucy, Jane Pearson; Frank Abbott, Jeremy Burnham; Judy Abbott, Ann Morrish; Mr Grieves, Stephen Yardley; Mrs Grieves, Christine Hargreaves; Mrs Roberts, Karin MacCarthy; Major Houghton, Norman Bird; Wendy, Alison Elliott.